Praise for *On Earth We're Briefly Gorgeous*

"Vuong as a writer is daring. . . . He transforms the emotional, the visceral, the individual into the political in an unforgettable—indeed, gorgeous—novel."
—Viet Thanh Nguyen, *Time*

"Vuong ties the private terrors of supposedly inconsequential people to the larger forces pulsing through America. . . . At times, the tension between Little Dog's passion and his concern seems to explode the very structure of traditional narrative, and the pages break apart into the lines of an evocative prose poem—not so much briefly gorgeous as permanently stunning."
—Ron Charles, *The Washington Post*

"Reading *On Earth We're Briefly Gorgeous* can feel like watching an act of endurance art, or a slow, strange piece of magic in which bones become sonatas, to borrow one of Vuong's metaphors."
—Jia Tolentino, *The New Yorker*

"Vuong is masterly at creating indelible, impressionistic images. . . . The book is brilliant in the way it pays attention not to what our thoughts make us feel, but to what our feelings make us think."
—*The New York Times Book Review*

NEW YORK TIMES BESTSELLER

Praise for *On Earth We're Briefly Gorgeous*

"Vuong writes about the yearning for connection that afflicts immigrants.
But 'ocean' also describes the distinctive way Vuong writes: His words are
liquid, flowing, rolling, teasing, mighty, and overpowering. When Vuong's
mother gave him the oh-so-apt name of Ocean, she inadvertently called
into being a writer whose language some of us readers could happily
drown in.... Like so many immigrant writers before him, Vuong has taken
the English he acquired with difficulty and not only made it his own—he's
made it better."   —Maureen Corrigan, *Fresh Air*

"A bildungsroman that vacillates between moments of piercing tenderness and savage brutality, set against quixotic hopes of the American
Dream and the devastation of the opioid crisis. Vuong's deeply felt work
might just be the first great fiction of this modern, homegrown travesty,
but it's also a story that is enriched by both the beautiful and the ugly currents of American history."   —Chloë Schama, Vogue.com

"Sometimes a writer comes along and stops your breath. I'm reading *On
Earth We're Briefly Gorgeous* and there is so little air moving through my
body as I read. When writing is *this* good, who needs air?"
                          —Jacqueline Woodson, author of *Red at the Bone*

"A bruised, breathtaking love letter never meant to be sent. A powerful
testimony to magic and loss. A marvel."
                          —Marlon James, author of *Black Leopard, Red Wolf*

"Ocean Vuong's devastatingly beautiful first novel, as evocative as its title, is a painful but extraordinary coming-of-age story about surviving the aftermath of trauma. . . . Vuong's language soars as he writes of beauty, survival, and freedom, which sometimes isn't freedom at all, but 'simply the cage widening far away from you, the bars abstracted with distance but still there.' . . . The title says it: Gorgeous."   —Heller McAlpin, NPR.org

"This is one of the best novels I've ever read. I always want my favorite poets to write novels and here it's happened. Ocean Vuong is a master. This book a masterpiece. *On Earth We're Briefly Gorgeous* is an ode to loss and struggle, to being a Vietnamese American, to Hartford, Connecticut, and it's a compassionate epistolary ode to a mother who may or may not know how to read. I dog-eared so many pages the book almost collapsed—I almost did."   —Tommy Orange, author of *There There*

"*On Earth We're Briefly Gorgeous* will be described—rightly—as luminous, shattering, urgent, necessary. But the word I keep circling back to is raw: that's how powerful the emotions here are, and how you'll feel after reading it—scoured down to bone. With a poet's precision, Ocean Vuong examines whether putting words to one's experience can bridge wounds that span generations, and whether it's ever possible to be truly heard by those we love most."   —Celeste Ng, author of *Everything I Never Told You* and *Little Fires Everywhere*

"This book—'gorgeous' is right there in the title—finds incredible, aching beauty in the deep observation of love in many forms. Ocean Vuong's debut novel contains all the power of his poetry, and I finished the book knowing that we are seeing only the very beginning of his truly magnificent talent."
—Emma Straub, author of *Modern Lovers* and *The Vacationers*

"Ocean Vuong runs up against the limits of language—this book is addressed to a mother who cannot read it—and expands our sense of what literature can make visible, thinkable, felt across borders and generations and genres. This is a courageous, embodied inquiry into the tangle of colonial and personal histories. It is also a gorgeous argument for astonishment over irony—for the transformative possibilities of love."

—Ben Lerner, author of *Leaving the Atocha Station* and *10:04*

"One is not often given the chance to apply words like 'brilliant' and 'remarkable' to any novels, certainly not first novels. Thank you, Ocean Vuong, for this brilliant and remarkable first novel."

—Michael Cunningham, author of *The Hours*

"[*On Earth We're Briefly Gorgeous*] is one of the most beautiful novels I have ever read, a literary marvel and a work of extraordinary humanity. It is about who we are, and how we find ourselves in our bodies, in each other, in countries, on this earth: truly a masterpiece."

—Max Porter, *Grief Is the Thing with Feathers*

To access Penguin Readers Guides online,
visit penguinrandomhouse.com.

on earth

we're briefly

gorgeous

A Novel

OCEAN VUONG

PENGUIN BOOKS

PENGUIN BOOKS
An imprint of Penguin Random House LLC
penguinrandomhouse.com

First published in the United States of America by Penguin Press,
an imprint of Penguin Random House LLC, 2019
Published in Penguin Books 2021

Portions of this book have previously appeared, in different form,
in *The New Yorker*, *Guernica*, and at Buzzfeed.com.

Excerpt from "Many Men (Wish Death)," words and music by Curtis Jackson, Luis Resto,
Keni St. Lewis, Frederick Perren, and Darrell Branch. Copyright © 2003 by Kobalt Music
Copyrights SARL, Resto World Music, Universal–Songs of PolyGram International, Inc.,
Bull Pen Music, Inc., Universal–PolyGram International Publishing, Inc., Perren-Vibes
Music, Inc., Figga Six Music and Unknown Publisher. All rights for Kobalt Music
Copyrights SARL and Resto World Music administered worldwide by Kobalt Songs
Music Publishing. All rights for Bull Pen Music, Inc., administered by Universal–Songs
of PolyGram International, Inc. All rights for Perren-Vibes Music, Inc., administered
by Universal–PolyGram International Publishing, Inc. All rights for Figga Six Music
administered by Downtown DMP Songs. All rights reserved. Used by permission.
Reprinted by permission of Hal Leonard LLC and Kobalt Music Services America Inc.
(KMSA) obo Resto World Music [ASCAP] Kobalt Music Services Ltd (KMS)
obo Kobalt Music Copyrights SARL.

ISBN 9780525562047 (paperback)

THE LIBRARY OF CONGRESS HAS CATALOGED THE HARDCOVER
EDITION AS FOLLOWS:
Names: Vuong, Ocean, 1988– author.
Title: On earth we're briefly gorgeous : a novel / Ocean Vuong.
Other titles: On earth we are briefly gorgeous
Description: New York : Penguin Press, 2019.
Identifiers: LCCN 2018046290 (print) | LCCN 2018050239 (ebook) |
ISBN 9780525562030 (ebook) | ISBN 9780525562023 (hardcover)
Subjects: | BISAC: Fiction / Literary. | Fiction / Cultural Heritage. |
Fiction / Coming of Age.
Classification: LCC PS3622.U96 (ebook) | LCC PS3622.U96 O52 2019 (print) |
DDC 813/.6—dc23
LC record available at https://lccn.loc.gov/2018046290

Printed in the United States of America
9th Printing

Book design by Daniel Lagin

For my mother

But let me see if—using these words as a little plot of
land and my life as a cornerstone—
I can build you a center.

—Qiu Miaojin

I want to tell you the truth, and already I have told you
about the wide rivers.

—Joan Didion

I

L et me begin again.

Dear Ma,

I am writing to reach you—even if each word I put down is one word further from where you are. I am writing to go back to the time, at the rest stop in Virginia, when you stared, horror-struck, at the taxidermy buck hung over the soda machine by the restrooms, its antlers shadowing your face. In the car, you kept shaking your head. "I don't understand why they would do that. Can't they see it's a corpse? A corpse should go away, not get stuck forever like that."

I think now of that buck, how you stared into its black glass eyes and saw your reflection, your whole body, warped in that lifeless mirror. How it was not the grotesque mounting of a decapitated animal that shook you—but that the taxidermy embodied a death that won't finish, a death that keeps dying as we walk past it to relieve ourselves.

I am writing because they told me to never start a sentence with *because*. But I wasn't trying to make a sentence—I was trying to break free. Because freedom, I am told, is nothing but the distance between the hunter and its prey.

Autumn. Somewhere over Michigan, a colony of monarch butterflies, numbering more than fifteen thousand, are beginning their yearly migration south. In the span of two months, from September to November, they will move, one wing beat at a time, from southern Canada and the United States to portions of central Mexico, where they will spend the winter.

They perch among us, on windowsills and chain-link fences, clotheslines still blurred from the just-hung weight of clothes, the hood of a faded-blue Chevy, their wings folding slowly, as if being put away, before snapping once, into flight.

It only takes a single night of frost to kill off a generation. To live, then, is a matter of time, of timing.

That time when I was five or six and, playing a prank, leapt out at you from behind the hallway door, shouting, "Boom!" You screamed, face raked and twisted, then burst into sobs, clutched your chest as you leaned against the door, gasping. I stood bewildered, my toy army helmet tilted on my head. I was an American boy parroting what I saw on TV. I didn't know that the war was still inside you, that there was a war to begin with, that once it enters you it never leaves—but merely echoes, a sound forming the face of your own son. Boom.

That time, in third grade, with the help of Mrs. Callahan, my ESL teacher, I read the first book that I loved, a children's book called *Thunder Cake,* by Patricia Polacco. In the story, when a girl and her grandmother spot a storm brewing on the green horizon, instead of shuttering the windows or nailing boards on the doors, they set out to bake a cake. I was unmoored by this act, its precarious yet bold refusal of common sense. As Mrs. Callahan stood behind me, her mouth at my ear, I was pulled deeper into the current of language. The story unfurled, its storm rolled in as she spoke, then rolled in once more as I repeated the words. To bake a cake in the eye of a storm; to feed yourself sugar on the cusp of danger.

The first time you hit me, I must have been four. A hand, a flash, a reckoning. My mouth a blaze of touch.

The time I tried to teach you to read the way Mrs. Callahan taught me, my lips to your ear, my hand on yours, the words moving underneath the shadows we made. But that act (a son teaching his mother) reversed our hierarchies, and with it our identities, which, in this country, were already tenuous and tethered. After the stutters and false starts, the sentences warped or locked in your throat, after the embarrassment of failure, you slammed the book shut. "I don't need to read," you said, your expression crunched, and pushed away from the table. "I can *see*—it's gotten me this far, hasn't it?"

Then the time with the remote control. A bruised welt on my forearm I would lie about to my teachers. "I fell playing tag."

The time, at forty-six, when you had a sudden desire to color. "Let's go to Walmart," you said one morning. "I need coloring books." For months, you filled the space between your arms with all the shades you couldn't pronounce. *Magenta, vermilion, marigold, pewter, juniper, cinnamon.* Each day, for hours, you slumped over landscapes of farms, pastures, Paris, two horses on a windswept plain, the face of a girl with black hair and skin you left blank, left white. You hung them all over the house, which started to resemble an elementary school classroom. When I asked you, "Why coloring, why now?" you put down the sapphire pencil and stared, dreamlike, at a half-finished garden. "I just go away in it for a while," you said, "but I feel everything. Like I'm still here, in this room."

The time you threw the box of Legos at my head. The hardwood dotted with blood.

"Have you ever made a scene," you said, filling in a Thomas Kinkade house, "and then put yourself inside it? Have you ever watched yourself from behind, going further and deeper into that landscape, away from you?"

How could I tell you that what you were describing was writing? How could I say that we, after all, are so close, the shadows of our hands, on two different pages, merging?

"I'm sorry," you said, bandaging the cut on my forehead. "Grab your coat. I'll get you McDonald's." Head throbbing, I dipped chicken nuggets in ketchup as you watched. "You have to get bigger and stronger, okay?"

I reread Roland Barthes's *Mourning Diary* yesterday, the book he wrote each day for a year after his mother's death. *I have known the body of my mother,* he writes, *sick and then dying.* And that's where I stopped. Where I decided to write to you. You who are still alive.

Those Saturdays at the end of the month when, if you had money left over after the bills, we'd go to the mall. Some people dressed up to go to church or dinner parties; we dressed to the nines to go to a commercial center off I-91. You would wake up early, spend an hour doing your makeup, put on your best sequined black dress, your one pair of gold hoop earrings, black lamé shoes. Then you would kneel and smear a handful of pomade through my hair, comb it over.

Seeing us there, a stranger couldn't tell that we bought our groceries at the local corner store on Franklin Avenue, where the doorway was littered with used food stamp receipts, where staples like milk and eggs cost three times more than they did in the suburbs, where the apples, wrinkled and bruised, lay in a cardboard box soaked on the bottom with pig's blood that had leaked from the crate of loose pork chops, the ice long melted.

"Let's get the fancy chocolates," you'd say, pointing to the Godiva chocolatier. We would get a small paper bag containing maybe five or six squares of chocolate we had picked at random. This was often all we bought at the mall. Then we'd walk, passing one back and forth until our fingers shone inky and sweet. "This is how you enjoy your life," you'd say, sucking your fingers, their pink nail polish chipped from a week of giving pedicures.

The time with your fists, shouting in the parking lot, the late sun etching your hair red. My arms shielding my head as your knuckles thudded around me.

Those Saturdays, we'd stroll the corridors until, one by one, the shops pulled shut their steel gates. Then we'd make our way to the bus stop down the street, our breaths floating above us, the makeup drying on your face. Our hands empty except for our hands.

Out my window this morning, just before sunrise, a deer stood in a fog so dense and bright that the second one, not too far away, looked like the unfinished shadow of the first.

You can color that in. You can call it "The History of Memory."

Migration can be triggered by the angle of sunlight, indicating a change in season, temperature, plant life, and food supply. Female monarchs lay eggs along the route. Every history has more than one thread, each thread a story of division. The journey takes four thousand eight hundred and thirty miles, more than the length of this country. The monarchs that fly south will not make it back north. Each departure, then, is final. Only their children return; only the future revisits the past.

What is a country but a borderless sentence, a life?

That time at the Chinese butcher, you pointed to the roasted pig hanging from its hook. "The ribs are just like a person's after they're burned." You let out a clipped chuckle, then paused, took out your pocketbook, your face pinched, and recounted our money.

What is a country but a life sentence?

The time with a gallon of milk. The jug bursting on my shoulder bone, then a steady white rain on the kitchen tiles.

The time at Six Flags, when you rode the Superman roller coaster with me because I was too scared to do it alone. How you threw up afterward, your whole head in the garbage can. How, in my screeching delight, I forgot to say *Thank you*.

The time we went to Goodwill and piled the cart with items that had a yellow tag, because on that day a yellow tag meant an additional fifty percent off. I pushed the cart and leaped on the back bar, gliding, feeling rich with our bounty of discarded treasures. It was your birthday. We were splurging. "Do I look like a real American?" you said, pressing a white dress to your length. It was slightly too formal for you to have any occasion to wear, yet casual enough to hold a *possibility* of use. A chance. I nodded, grinning. The cart was so full by then I no longer saw what was ahead of me.

The time with the kitchen knife—the one you picked up, then put down, shaking, saying quietly, "Get out. Get out." And I ran out the door, down the black summer streets. I ran until I forgot I was ten, until my heartbeat was all I could hear of myself.

The time, in New York City, a week after cousin Phuong died in the car wreck, I stepped onto the uptown 2 train and saw his face, clear and round as the doors opened, looking right at me, alive. I gasped—but knew better, that it was only a man who resembled him. Still, it upended me to see what I thought I'd never see again— the features so exact, heavy jaw, open brow. His name lunged to the fore of my mouth before I caught it. Aboveground, I sat on a hydrant and called you. "Ma, I saw him," I breathed. "Ma, I swear I saw him. I know it's stupid but I saw Phuong on the train." I was having a panic attack. And you knew it. For a while you said nothing, then started to hum the melody to "Happy Birthday." It was not my birthday but it was the only song you knew in English, and you kept going. And I listened, the phone pressed so hard to my ear that, hours later, a pink rectangle was still imprinted on my cheek.

I am twenty-eight years old, 5ft 4in tall, 112lbs. I am handsome at exactly three angles and deadly from everywhere else. I am writing you from inside a body that used to be yours. Which is to say, I am writing as a son.

If we are lucky, the end of the sentence is where we might begin. If we are lucky, something is passed on, another alphabet written in the blood, sinew, and neuron; ancestors charging their kin with the silent propulsion to fly south, to turn toward the place in the narrative no one was meant to outlast.

———

The time, at the nail salon, I overheard you consoling a customer over her recent loss. While you painted her nails, she spoke, between tears. "I lost my baby, my little girl, Julie. I can't believe it, she was my strongest, my oldest."

You nodded, eyes sober behind your mask. "It's okay, it's okay," you said in English, "don't cry. Your Julie," you went on, "how she die?"

"Cancer," the lady said. "And in the backyard, too! She died right there in the backyard, dammit."

You put down her hand, took off your mask. Cancer. You leaned forward. "My mom, too, she die from the cancer." The room went quiet. Your co-workers shifted in their seats. "But what happen in backyard, why she die there?"

The woman wiped her eyes. "That's where she lives. Julie's my horse."

You nodded, put on your mask, and got back to painting her nails. After the woman left, you flung the mask across the room. "A fucking horse?" you said in Vietnamese. "Holy shit, I was ready to go to her daughter's grave with flowers!" For the rest of the day, while you worked on one hand or another, you would look up and shout, "It was a fucking horse!" and we'd all laugh.

The time, at thirteen, when I finally said stop. Your hand in the air, my cheek bone stinging from the first blow. "Stop, Ma. Quit it. Please." I looked at you hard, the way I had learned, by then, to look into the eyes of my bullies. You turned away and, saying nothing, put on your brown wool coat and walked to the store. "I'm getting eggs," you said over your shoulder, as if nothing had happened. But we both knew you'd never hit me again.

Monarchs that survived the migration passed this message down to their children. The memory of family members lost from the initial winter was woven into their genes.

When does a war end? When can I say your name and have it mean only your name and not what you left behind?

The time I woke into an ink-blue hour, my head—no, the house—filled with soft music. My feet on cool hardwood, I walked to your room. Your bed was empty. "Ma," I said, still as a cut flower over the music. It was Chopin, and it was coming from the closet. The door etched in reddish light, like the entrance to a place on fire. I sat outside it, listening to the overture and, underneath that, your steady breathing. I don't know how long I was there. But at one point I went back to bed, pulled the covers to my chin until it stopped, not the song but my shaking. "Ma," I said again, to no one, "come back. Come back out."

You once told me that the human eye is god's loneliest creation. How so much of the world passes through the pupil and still it holds nothing. The eye, alone in its socket, doesn't even know there's another one, just like it, an inch away, just as hungry, as empty. Opening the front door to the first snowfall of my life, you whispered, "Look."

The time, while pruning a basket of green beans over the sink, you said, out of nowhere, "I'm not a monster. I'm a mother."

What do we mean when we say survivor? Maybe a survivor is the last one to come home, the final monarch that lands on a branch already weighted with ghosts.

The morning closed in around us.

I put down the book. The heads of the green beans went on snapping. They thunked in the steel sink like fingers. "You're not a monster," I said.

But I lied.

What I really wanted to say was that a monster is not such a terrible thing to be. From the Latin root *monstrum*, a divine messenger of catastrophe, then adapted by the Old French to mean an animal of myriad origins: centaur, griffin, satyr. To be a monster is to be a hybrid signal, a lighthouse: both shelter and warning at once.

I read that parents suffering from PTSD are more likely to hit their children. Perhaps there is a monstrous origin to it, after all. Perhaps to lay hands on your child is to prepare him for war. To say possessing a heartbeat is never as simple as the heart's task of saying *yes yes yes* to the body.

I don't know.

What I do know is that back at Goodwill you handed me the white dress, your eyes glazed and wide. "Can you read this," you said, "and tell me if it's fireproof?" I searched the hem, studied the print on the tag, and, not yet able to read myself, said, "Yeah." Said it anyway. "Yeah," I lied, holding the dress up to your chin. "It's fireproof."

Days later, a neighborhood boy, riding by on his bike, would see me wearing that very dress—I had put it on thinking I would look more like you—in the front yard while you were at work. At recess the next day, the kids would call me *freak, fairy, fag.* I would learn, much later, that those words were also iterations of *monster.*

Sometimes, I imagine the monarchs fleeing not winter but the napalm clouds of your childhood in Vietnam. I imagine them flying from the blazed blasts unscathed, their tiny black-and-red wings jittering like debris that kept blowing, for thousands of miles across the sky, so that, looking up, you can no longer fathom the explosion they came from, only a family of butterflies floating in clean, cool air, their wings finally, after so many conflagrations, fireproof.

"That's so good to know, baby." You stared off, stone-faced, over my shoulder, the dress held to your chest. "That's so good."

You're a mother, Ma. You're also a monster. But so am I— which is why I can't turn away from you. Which is why I have taken god's loneliest creation and put you inside it.

Look.

In a previous draft of this letter, one I've since deleted, I told you how I came to be a writer. How I, the first in our family to go to college, squandered it on a degree in English. How I fled my shitty high school to spend my days in New York lost in library stacks, reading obscure texts by dead people, most of whom never dreamed a face like mine floating over their sentences—and least of all that those sentences would save me. But none of that matters now. What matters is that all of it, even if I didn't know it then, brought me here, to this page, to tell you everything you'll never know.

What happened was that I was a boy once and bruiseless. I was eight when I stood in the one-bedroom apartment in Hartford staring at Grandma Lan's sleeping face. Despite being your mother, she is nothing like you; her skin three shades darker, the color of dirt after a rainstorm, spread over a skeletal face whose eyes shone like chipped glass. I can't say what made me leave the green pile of army men and walk over to where she lay under a blanket on the hardwood, arms folded across her chest. Her eyes moved behind their lids as she slept. Her forehead, lashed deep with lines, marked her fifty-six years. A fly landed on the side of her mouth, then skittered to the edge of her purplish lips. Her left cheek spasmed a few seconds. The skin, pocked with large black pores, rippled in the sunlight. I had never seen so much movement in sleep before—except in dogs who run in dreams none of us will ever know.

But it was stillness, I realize now, that I sought, not of her body, which kept ticking as she slept, but of her mind. Only in this twitching quiet did her brain, wild and explosive during waking hours, cool itself into something like calm. I'm watching a stranger, I thought, one whose lips creased into an expression of contentment alien to the Lan I knew awake, the one whose sentences rambled and rattled out of her, her schizophrenia only worse now since the war. But wildness is how I had always known her. Ever since I could remember, she flickered before me, dipping in and out of sense. Which was why, studying her now, tranquil in the afternoon light, was like looking back in time.

The eye opened. Glazed by a milky film of sleep, it widened to hold my image. I stood against myself, pinned by the shaft of light through the window. Then the second eye opened, this one slightly pink but clearer. "You hungry, Little Dog?" she asked, her face expressionless, as if still asleep.

I nodded.

"What should we eat in a time like this?" She gestured around the room.

A rhetorical question, I decided, and bit my lip.

But I was wrong. "I said *What* can we eat?" She sat up, her shoulder-length hair splayed out behind her like a cartoon character just blasted with TNT. She crawled over, squatted before the toy army men, picked one up from the pile, pinched it between her fingers, and studied it. Her nails, perfectly painted and manicured by you, with your usual precision, were the only unblemished thing about her. Decorous and ruby-glossed, they stood out from her callused and chapped knuckles as she held the soldier, a radio operator, and examined it as though a newly unearthed artifact.

A radio mounted to his back, the soldier crouches on one knee, shouting forever into the receiver. His attire suggests he's fighting in WWII. "Who yoo arrgh, messeur?" she asked the plastic man in broken English and French. In one jerking motion, she pressed his radio to her ear and listened intently, her eyes on me. "You know what they telling me, Little Dog?" she whispered in Vietnamese. "They say—" She dipped her head to one side, leaned in to me, her breath a mix of Ricola cough drops and the meaty scent of sleep, the little green man's head swallowed by her ear. "They say good soldiers only win when their grandmas feed them." She let out a single, clipped cackle—then stopped, her expression suddenly blank, and placed the radio man in my hand, closed it into a fist. Like that she rose and shuffled off to the kitchen, her sandals clapping behind her. I clutched the message, the plastic antennae stabbing my palm as the sound of reggae, muffled through a neighbor's wall, seeped into the room.

I have and have had many names. Little Dog was what Lan called me. What made a woman who named herself and her daughter after flowers call her grandson a dog? A woman who watches out for her own, that's who. As you know, in the village where Lan grew up, a child, often the smallest or weakest of the flock, as I was, is named after the most despicable things: demon, ghost child, pig snout, monkey-born, buffalo head, bastard—little dog being the more tender one. Because evil spirits, roaming the land for healthy, beautiful children, would hear the name of something hideous and ghastly being called in for supper and pass over the house, sparing the child. To love something, then, is to name it after something so worthless it might be left untouched— and alive. A name, thin as air, can also be a shield. A Little Dog shield.

I sat on the kitchen tiles and watched Lan scoop two steaming mounds of rice into a porcelain bowl rimmed with painted indigo vines. She grabbed a teapot and poured a stream of jasmine tea over the rice, just enough for a few grains to float in the pale amber liquid. Sitting on the floor, we passed the fragrant, steaming bowl between us. It tasted the way you'd imagine mashed flowers would taste—bitter and dry, with a bright and sweet aftertaste. "True peasant food." Lan grinned. "This is our fast food, Little Dog. This is our McDonald's!" She tilted to one side and let out a huge fart. I followed her lead and let one go myself, prompting us to both laugh with our eyes closed. Then she stopped. "Finish it." She pointed with her chin at the bowl. "Every grain of rice you leave behind is one maggot you eat in hell." She removed the rubber band from her wrist and tied her hair in a bun.

They say that trauma affects not only the brain, but the body too, its musculature, joints, and posture. Lan's back was perpetually bent—so much so that I could barely see her head as she stood at the sink. Only the knot of tied-back hair was visible, bobbing as she scrubbed.

She glanced at the pantry shelf, empty save for a lone half-eaten jar of peanut butter. "I have to buy more bread."

One night, a day or two before Independence Day, the neighbors were shooting fireworks from a rooftop down the block. Phosphorescent streaks raked up the purple, light-polluted sky and shredded into huge explosions that reverberated through our apartment. I was asleep on the living room floor, wedged between you and Lan, when I felt the warmth of her body, which was pressed all night against my back, vanish. When I turned, she was on her knees, scratching wildly at the blankets. Before I could ask what was wrong, her hand, cold and wet, grabbed my mouth. She placed her finger over her lips.

"Shhh. If you scream," I heard her say, "the mortars will know where we are."

The streetlight in her eyes reflecting jaundiced pools on her dark face. She grabbed my wrist and pulled me toward the window, where we crouched, huddled under the sill, listening to the bangs ricochet above us. Slowly, she guided me into her lap and we waited.

She went on, in whispered bursts, about the mortars, her hand periodically covering my lower face—the scent of garlic and Tiger Balm sharp in my nose. We must have sat for two hours like that, her heartbeat steady on my back as the room began to grey, then washed in indigo, revealing two sleeping forms swaddled in blankets and stretched across the floor before us: you and your sister, Mai. You resembled soft mountain ranges on a snowy tundra. My family, I thought, was this silent arctic landscape, placid at last after a night of artillery fire. When Lan's chin grew heavy on my shoulder, her exhales evening out in my ear, I knew she had finally joined her daughters in sleep, and the snow in July—smooth, total, and nameless—was all I could see.

Before I was Little Dog, I had another name—the name I was born with. One October afternoon in a banana-thatched hut outside Saigon, on the same rice paddy you grew up on, I became your son. As Lan told it, a local shaman and his two assistants squatted outside the hut waiting for the first cries. After Lan and the midwives cut the umbilical cord, the shaman and his helpers rushed in, wrapped me, still sticky with birth, in a white cloth, and raced to the nearby river, where I was bathed under veils of incense smoke and sage.

Screaming, ash smudged across my forehead, I was placed in my father's arms and the shaman whispered the name he had given me. It means Patriotic Leader of the Nation, the shaman explained. Having been hired by my father, and noticing my old man's gruff demeanor, the way he puffed out his chest to widen his 5ft-2in frame as he walked, speaking with gestures that resembled blows, the shaman picked a name, I imagine, that would satisfy the man who paid him. And he was right. My father beamed, Lan said, lifting me over his head at the hut's threshold. "My son will be the leader of Vietnam," he shouted. But in two years, Vietnam—which, thirteen years after the war and still in shambles—would grow so dire that we would flee the very ground he stood on, the soil where, a few feet away, your blood had made a dark red circle between your legs, turning the dirt there into fresh mud—and I was alive.

Other times, Lan seemed ambivalent to noise. Do you remember that one night, after we had gathered around Lan to hear a story after dinner, and the gunshots started firing off across the street? Although gunshots were not uncommon in Hartford, I was never prepared for the sound—piercing yet somehow more mundane than I imagined, like little league home runs cracked one after another out of the night's park. We all screamed—you, Aunt Mai, and I—our cheeks and noses pressed to the floor. "Someone turn off the lights," you shouted.

After the room went black for a few seconds, Lan said, "What? It's only three shots." Her voice came from the exact place where she was sitting. She hadn't even flinched. "Is it not? Are you dead or are you breathing?"

Her clothes rustled against her skin as she waved us over. "In the war, entire villages would go up before you know where your balls were." She blew her nose. "Now turn the light back on before I forget where I left off."

With Lan, one of my tasks was to take a pair of tweezers and pluck, one by one, the grey hairs from her head. "The snow in my hair," she explained, "it makes my head itch. Will you pluck my itchy hairs, Little Dog? The snow is rooting into me." She slid a pair of tweezers between my fingers, "Make Grandma young today, okay?" she said real quiet, grinning.

For this work I was paid in stories. After positioning her head under the window's light, I would kneel on a pillow behind her, the tweezers ready in my grip. She would start to talk, her tone dropping an octave, drifting deep into a narrative. Mostly, as was her way, she rambled, the tales cycling one after another. They spiraled out from her mind only to return the next week with the same introduction: "Now this one, Little Dog, this one will *really* take you out. You ready? Are you even interested in what I'm saying? Good. Because I never lie." A familiar story would follow, punctuated with the same dramatic pauses and inflections during moments of suspense or crucial turns. I'd mouth along with the sentences, as if watching a film for the umpteenth time—a movie made by Lan's words and animated by my imagination. In this way, we collaborated.

As I plucked, the blank walls around us did not so much fill with fantastical landscapes as open into them, the plaster disintegrating to reveal the past behind it. Scenes from the war, mythologies of manlike monkeys, of ancient ghost catchers from the hills of Da Lat who were paid in jugs of rice wine, who traveled through villages with packs of wild dogs and spells written on palm leaves to dispel evil spirits.

There were personal stories too. Like the time she told of how you were born, of the white American serviceman deployed on a navy destroyer in Cam Ranh Bay. How Lan met him wearing her purple áo dài, the split sides billowing behind her under the bar lights as she walked. How, by then, she had already left her first husband from an arranged marriage. How, as a young woman living in a wartime city for the first time with no family, it was her body, her purple dress, that kept her alive. As she spoke, my hand slowed, then stilled. I was engrossed in the film playing across the apartment walls. I had forgotten myself into her story, had lost my way, willingly, until she reached back and swatted my thigh. "Hey, don't you sleep on me now!" But I wasn't asleep. I was standing next to her as her purple dress swayed in the smoky bar, the glasses clinking under the scent of motor oil and cigars, of vodka and gunsmoke from the soldiers' uniforms.

"Help me, Little Dog." She pressed my hands to her chest. "Help me stay young, get this snow off of my life—get it all off my life." I came to know, in those afternoons, that madness can sometimes lead to discovery, that the mind, fractured and short-wired, is not entirely wrong. The room filled and refilled with our voices as the snow fell from her head, the hardwood around my knees whitening as the past unfolded around us.

And then there was the school bus. That morning, like all mornings, no one sat next to me. I pressed myself against the window and filled my vision with the outside, mauve with early dark: the Motel 6, the Kline's Laundromat, not yet opened, a beige and hoodless Toyota stranded in a front yard with a tire swing half tilted in dirt. As the bus sped up, bits of the city whirled by like objects in a washing machine. All around me the boys jostled each other. I felt the wind from their quick-jerked limbs behind my neck, their swooping arms and fists displacing the air. Knowing the face I possess, its rare features in these parts, I pushed my head harder against the window to avoid them. That's when I saw a spark in the middle of a parking lot outside. It wasn't until I heard their voices behind me that I realized the spark came from inside my head. That someone had shoved my face into the glass.

"Speak English," said the boy with a yellow bowl cut, his jowls flushed and rippling.

The cruelest walls are made of glass, Ma. I had the urge to break through the pane and leap out the window.

"Hey." The jowlboy leaned in, his vinegar mouth on the side of my cheek. "Don't you ever say nothin'? Don't you speak English?" He grabbed my shoulder and spun me to face him. "Look at me when I'm talking to you."

He was only nine but had already mastered the dialect of damaged American fathers. The boys crowded around me, sensing entertainment. I could smell their fresh-laundered clothes, the lavender and lilac in the softeners.

They waited to see what would happen. When I did nothing but close my eyes, the boy slapped me.

"Say something." He shoved his fleshy nose against my blazed cheek. "Can't you say even *one* thing?"

The second slap came from above, from another boy.

Bowlcut cupped my chin and steered my head toward him.

"Say my name then." He blinked, his eyelashes, long and blond, nearly nothing, quivered. "Like your mom did last night."

Outside, the leaves fell, fat and wet as dirty money, across the windows. I willed myself into a severe obedience and said his name.

I let their laughter enter me.

"Again," he said.

"Kyle."

"Louder."

"Kyle." My eyes still shut.

"That's a good little bitch."

Then, like a break in weather, a song came on the radio. "Hey, my cousin just went to their concert!" And like that it was over. Their shadows cleared above me. I let my nose drip with snot. I stared at my feet, at the shoes you bought me, the ones with red lights that flashed on the soles when I walked.

My forehead pressed to the seat in front of me, I kicked my shoes, gently at first, then faster. My sneakers erupted with silent flares: the world's smallest ambulances, going nowhere.

That night you were sitting on the couch with a towel wrapped around your head after your shower, a Marlboro Red smoldering in your hand. I stood there, holding myself.

"Why?" You stared hard at the TV.

You stabbed the cigarette into your teacup and I immediately regretted saying anything. "Why'd you let them do that? Don't close your eyes. You're not sleepy."

You put your eyes on me, blue smoke swirling between us.

"What kind of boy would let them do that?" Smoke leaked from the corners of your mouth. "You did nothing." You shrugged. "Just let them."

I thought of the window again, how everything seemed like a window, even the air between us.

You grabbed my shoulders, your forehead pressed fast to my own. "Stop crying. You're always crying!" You were so close I could smell the ash and toothpaste between your teeth. "Nobody touched you yet. Stop crying—I said stop, dammit!"

The third slap that day flung my gaze to one side, the TV screen flashed before my head snapped back to face you. Your eyes darted back and forth across my face.

Then you pulled me into you, my chin pressed hard to your shoulder.

"You have to find a way, Little Dog," you said into my hair. "You have to because I don't have the English to help you. I can't say nothing to stop them. You find a way. You find a way or you don't tell me about this ever again, you hear?" You pulled back. "You have to be a real boy and be strong. You have to step up or they'll keep going. You have a bellyful of English." You placed your palm on my stomach, almost whispering, "You have to use it, okay?"

"Yes, Ma."

You brushed my hair to one side, kissed my forehead. You studied me, a bit too long, before falling back on the sofa waving your hand. "Get me another cigarette."

When I came back with the Marlboro and a Zippo lighter, the TV was off. You just sat there staring out the blue window.

The next morning, in the kitchen, I watched as you poured the milk into a glass tall as my head.

"Drink," you said, your lips pouted with pride. "This is American milk so you're gonna grow a lot. No doubt about it."

I drank so much of that cold milk it grew tasteless on my numbed tongue. Each morning after that, we'd repeat this ritual: the milk poured with a thick white braid, I'd drink it down, gulping, making sure you could see, both of us hoping the whiteness vanishing into me would make more of a yellow boy.

I'm drinking light, I thought. I'm filling myself with light. The milk would erase all the dark inside me with a flood of brightness. "A little more," you said, rapping the counter. "I know it's a lot. But it's worth it."

I clanked the glass down on the counter, beaming. "See?" you said, arms crossed. "You already look like Superman!"

I grinned, milk bubbling between my lips.

Some people say history moves in a spiral, not the line we have come to expect. We travel through time in a circular trajectory, our distance increasing from an epicenter only to return again, one circle removed.

Lan, through her stories, was also traveling in a spiral. As I listened, there would be moments when the story would change—not much, just a minuscule detail, the time of day, the color of someone's shirt, two air raids instead of three, an AK-47 instead of a 9mm, the daughter laughing, not crying. Shifts in the narrative would occur—the past never a fixed and dormant landscape but one that is re-seen. Whether we want to or not, we are traveling in a spiral, we are creating something new from what is gone. "Make me young again," Lan said. "Make me black again, not snow like this, Little Dog. Not snow."

But the truth is I don't know, Ma. I have theories I write down then erase and walk away from the desk. I put the kettle on and let the sound of boiling water change my mind. What's your theory—about anything? I know if I asked you, you'd laugh, covering your mouth, a gesture common among the girls in your childhood village, one you've kept all your life, even with your naturally straight teeth. You'd say no, theories are for people with too much time and not enough determination. But I know of one.

We were on a plane to California—do you remember this? You were giving him, my father, another chance, even with your nose still crooked from his countless backhands. I was six and we had left Lan behind in Hartford with Mai. At one point on the flight, the turbulence got so bad I bounced on the seat, my entire tiny self lifted clean off the cushion, then yanked down by the seatbelt. I started to cry. You wrapped one arm around my shoulders, leaned in, your weight absorbing the plane's throttle. Then you pointed to the thick cloud-bands outside the window and said, "When we get this high up, the clouds turn into boulders—hard rocks—that's what you're feeling." Your lips grazing my ear, your tone soothing,

I examined the massive granite-colored mountains across the sky's horizon. Yes, of course the plane shook. We were moving through rocks, our flight a supernatural perseverance of passage. Because to go back to that man took that kind of magic. The plane *should* rattle, it should nearly shatter. With the laws of the universe made new, I sat back and watched as we broke through one mountain after another.

When it comes to words, you possess fewer than the coins you saved from your nail salon tips in the milk gallon under the kitchen cabinet. Often you'd gesture to a bird, a flower, or a pair of lace curtains from Walmart and say only that it's beautiful—whatever it was. "Đẹp quá!" you once exclaimed, pointing to the hummingbird whirring over the creamy orchid in the neighbor's yard. "It's beautiful!" You asked me what it was called and I answered in English—the only language I had for it. You nodded blankly.

The next day, you had already forgotten the name, the syllables slipping right from your tongue. But then, coming home from town, I spotted the hummingbird feeder in our front yard, the glass orb filled with a clear, sweet nectar, surrounded by colorful plastic blossoms with pinhead holes for their beaks. When I asked you about it, you pulled the crumpled cardboard box from the garbage, pointed to the hummingbird, its blurred wings and needled beak—a bird you could not name but could nonetheless recognize. "Đẹp quá," you smiled. "Đẹp quá."

When you came home that night, after Lan and I had eaten our share of tea-rice, we all walked the forty minutes it took to get to the C-Town off New Britain Avenue. It was near closing and the aisles were empty. You wanted to buy oxtail, to make bún bò huế for the cold winter week ahead of us.

Lan and I stood beside you at the butcher counter, holding hands, as you searched the blocks of marbled flesh in the glass case. Not seeing the tails, you waved to the man behind the counter. When he asked if he could help, you paused for too long before saying, in Vietnamese, "Đuôi bò. Anh có đuôi bò không?"

His eyes flicked over each of our faces and asked again, leaning closer. Lan's hand twitched in my grip. Floundering, you placed your index finger at the small of your back, turned slightly, so the man could see your backside, then wiggled your finger while making mooing sounds. With your other hand, you made a pair of horns above your head. You moved, carefully twisting and gyrating so he could recognize each piece of this performance: horns, tail, ox. But he only laughed, his hand over his mouth at first, then louder, booming. The sweat on your forehead caught the fluorescent light. A middle-aged woman, carrying a box of Lucky Charms, shuffled past us, suppressing a smile. You worried a molar with your tongue, your cheek bulging. You were drowning, it seemed, in air. You tried French, pieces of which remained from your childhood. "Derrière de vache!" you shouted, the veins in your neck showing. By way of reply the man called to the back room, where a shorter man with darker features emerged and spoke to you in Spanish. Lan dropped my hand and joined you—mother and daughter twirling and mooing in circles, Lan giggling the whole time.

The men roared, slapping the counter, their teeth showing huge and white. You turned to me, your face wet, pleading. "Tell them. Go ahead and tell them what we need." I didn't know that oxtail was called *oxtail*. I shook my head, shame welling inside me. The men stared, their chortling now reduced to bewildered concern. The store was closing. One of them asked again, head lowered, sincere. But we turned from them. We abandoned the oxtail, the bún bò huế. You grabbed a loaf of Wonder Bread and a jar of mayonnaise. None of us spoke as we checked out, our words suddenly wrong everywhere, even in our mouths.

In line, among the candy bars and magazines, was a tray of mood rings. You picked one up between your fingers and, after checking the price, took three—one for each of us. "Đẹp quá," you said after a while, barely audible. "Đẹp quá."

No object is in a constant relationship with pleasure, wrote Barthes. *For the writer, however, it is the mother tongue.* But what if the mother tongue is stunted? What if that tongue is not only the symbol of a void, but is itself a void, what if the tongue is cut out? Can one take pleasure in loss without losing oneself entirely? The Vietnamese I own is the one you gave me, the one whose diction and syntax reach only the second-grade level.

As a girl, you watched, from a banana grove, your schoolhouse collapse after an American napalm raid. At five, you never stepped into a classroom again. Our mother tongue, then, is no mother at all—but an orphan. Our Vietnamese a time capsule, a mark of where your education ended, ashed. Ma, to speak in our mother tongue is to speak only partially in Vietnamese, but entirely in war.

That night I promised myself I'd never be wordless when you needed me to speak for you. So began my career as our family's official interpreter. From then on, I would fill in our blanks, our silences, stutters, whenever I could. I code switched. I took off our language and wore my English, like a mask, so that others would see my face, and therefore yours.

When you worked for a year at the clock factory, I called your boss and said, in my most polite diction, that my mother would like her hours reduced. Why? Because she was exhausted, because she was falling asleep in the bathtub after she came home from work, and that I was afraid she would drown. A week later your hours were cut. Or the times, so many times, I would call the Victoria's Secret catalog, ordering you bras, underwear, leggings. How the call ladies, after confusion from the prepubescent voice on the other end, relished in a boy buying lingerie for his mother. They awww'd into the phone, often throwing in free shipping. And they would ask me about school, cartoons I was watching, they would tell me about their own sons, that you, my mother, must be so happy.

I don't know if you're happy, Ma. I never asked.

Back in the apartment, we had no oxtail. But we *did* have three mood rings, one glinting on each of our fingers. You were lying facedown on a blanket spread on the floor with Lan straddled across your back, kneading the knots and stiff cords from your shoulders. The greenish TV light made us all seem underwater. Lan was mumbling another monologue from one of her lives, each sentence a remix of the last, and interrupted herself only to ask you where it hurt.

Two languages cancel each other out, suggests Barthes, beckoning a third. Sometimes our words are few and far between, or simply ghosted. In which case the hand, although limited by the borders of skin and cartilage, can be that third language that animates where the tongue falters.

It's true that, in Vietnamese, we rarely say *I love you,* and when we do, it is almost always in English. Care and love, for us, are pronounced clearest through service: plucking white hairs, pressing yourself on your son to absorb a plane's turbulence and, therefore, his fear. Or now—as Lan called to me, "Little Dog, get over here and help me help your mother." And we knelt on each side of you, rolling out the hardened cords in your upper arms, then down to your wrists, your fingers. For a moment almost too brief to matter, this made sense—that three people on the floor, connected to each other by touch, made something like the word *family.*

You groaned with relief as we worked your muscles loose, unraveling you with nothing but our own weight. You lifted your finger and, speaking into the blanket, said, "Am I happy?"

It wasn't until I saw the mood ring that I realized you were asking me, once more, to interpret another portion of America. Before I could answer, Lan thrust her hand before my nose. "Check me too, Little Dog—am I happy?" It could be, in writing you here, I am writing to everyone—for how can there be a private space if there is no safe space, if a boy's name can both shield him and turn him into an animal at once?

"Yes. You're both happy," I answered, knowing nothing. "You're both happy, Ma. Yes," I said again. Because gunshots, lies, and oxtail—or whatever you want to call your god—should say *Yes* over and over, in cycles, in spirals, with no other reason but to hear itself exist. Because love, at its best, repeats itself. Shouldn't it?

"I'm happy!" Lan threw her arms in the air. "I'm happy on my boat. My boat, see?" She pointed to your arms, splayed out like oars, she and I on each side. I looked down and saw it, the brown, yellowish floorboards swirling into muddy currents. I saw the weak ebb thick with grease and dead grass. We weren't rowing, but adrift. We were clinging to a mother the size of a raft until the mother beneath us grew stiff with sleep. And we soon fell silent as the raft took us all down this great brown river called America, finally happy.

It is a beautiful country depending on where you look. Depending on where you look you might see the woman waiting on the shoulder of the dirt road, an infant girl wrapped in a sky-blue shawl in her arms. She rocks her hips, cups the girl's head. *You were born,* the woman thinks, *because no one else was coming.* Because no one else is coming, she begins to hum.

A woman, not yet thirty, clutches her daughter on the shoulder of a dirt road in a beautiful country where two men, M-16s in their hands, step up to her. She is at a checkpoint, a gate made of concertina and weaponized permission. Behind her, the fields have begun to catch. A braid of smoke through a page-blank sky. One man has black hair, the other a yellow mustache like a scar of sunlight. Stench of gasoline coming off their fatigues. The rifles sway as they walk up to her, their metal bolts winking in afternoon sun.

A woman, a girl, a gun. This is an old story, one anyone can tell. A trope in a movie you can walk away from if it weren't already here, already written down.

It has started to rain; the dirt around the woman's bare feet is flecked with red-brown quotation marks—her body a thing spoken with. Her white shirt clings against her bony shoulders as she sweats. The grass all around her is flattened, as if god had pressed his hand there, reserving a space for an eighth day. It's a beautiful country, she's been told, depending on who you are.

It's not a god—of course not—but a helicopter, a Huey, another lord whose wind's so heavy that, a few feet away, a lint-grey warbler thrashes in the high grass, unable to correct herself.

The girl's eye fills with the chopper in the sky, her face a dropped peach. Her blue shawl finally made visible with black ink, like this.

Somewhere, deep inside this beautiful country, in the back of a garage lit with a row of fluorescent lights, as legend has it, five men have gathered around a table. Beneath their sandaled feet, pools of motor oil reflect nothing. On one end of the table a cluster of glass bottles. The vodka inside them shimmers in the harsh light as the men talk, their elbows shifting impatiently. They fall silent each time one of them glances toward the door. It should open anytime now. The light flickers once, stays on.

The vodka poured into shot glasses, some ringed with rust from being stored in a metal bullet case from the previous war. The heavy glasses *thunk* on the table, the burn swallowed into a darkness invented by thirst.

If I say the woman. If I say the woman is bearing down, her back hunched below this man-made storm, would you see her? From where you are standing, inches, which is to say years, from this page, would you see the shred of blue shawl blowing across her collarbones, the mole at the outside corner of her left eye as she squints at the men, who are now close enough for her to realize they are not men at all, but boys—eighteen, twenty at most? Can you hear the sound of the chopper, its dismemberment of air so loud it drowns the shouting beneath it? The wind coarse with smoke—and something else, a sweat-soaked char, its odd and acrid taste blowing from a hut at the edge of the field. A hut that, moments ago, was filled with human voices.

The girl, her ear pressed to the woman's chest, listens as if eavesdropping behind a door. There is something running inside the woman, a beginning, or rather, a rearranging of syntax. Eyes closed, she searches, her tongue on the cliff of a sentence.

The veins green over his wrists, the boy raises the M-16, blond hairs sweated brown along his arms. The men are drinking and laughing, their gapped teeth like mouthfuls of dice. This boy, his lips pulled at an angle, green eyes filmed pink. This private first class. The men are ready to forget, a few still have the scent of their wives' makeup on their fingers. His mouth opens and closes rapidly. He is asking a question, or questions, he is turning the air around his words into weather. Is there a language for falling out of language? A flash of teeth, a finger on the trigger, the boy saying, "No. No, step back."

The olive tag stitched to the boy's chest frames a word. Although the woman cannot read it, she knows it signals a name, something given by a mother or father, something weightless yet carried forever, like a heartbeat. She knows the first letter in the name is C. Like in Go Cong, the name of the open-air market she had visited two days ago, its neon marquee buzzing at the entrance. She was there to buy a new shawl for the girl. The cloth had cost more than what she had planned to spend, but when she saw it, day-bright among the grey and brown bolts, she peered up at the sky, even though it was already nightfall, and paid knowing there would be nothing left to eat with. Sky blue.

When the door opens, the men put down their glasses, some after quickly draining the dregs. A macaque monkey, the size of a dog, is led, with collar and leash, by a stooped man with combed white hair. No one speaks. All ten eyes are on the mammal as it staggers into the room, its burnt-red hair reeking of alcohol and feces, having been force-fed vodka and morphine in its cage all morning.

The fluorescent hums steady above them, as if the scene is a dream the light is having.

A woman stands on the shoulder of a dirt road begging, in a tongue made obsolete by gunfire, to enter the village where her house sits, has sat for decades. It is a human story. Anyone can tell it. Can you tell? Can you tell the rain has grown heavy, its keystrokes peppering the blue shawl black?

The force of the soldier's voice pushes the woman back. She wavers, one arm flailing, then steadies, pressing the girl into her.

A mother and a daughter. A me and a you. It's an old story.

The stooped man leads the monkey under the table, guides its head through a hole cut in the center. Another bottle is opened. The twist cap clicks as the men reach for their glasses.

The monkey is tied to a beam under the table. It jostles about. With its mouth muffled behind a leather strap, its screams sound more like the reel of a fishing rod cast far across a pond.

Seeing the letters on the boy's chest, the woman remembers her own name. The possession of a name, after all, being all they share.

"Lan," she says. "Tên tôi là Lan." My name is Lan.

Lan meaning Orchid. Lan the name she gave herself, having been born nameless. Because her mother simply called her *Seven*, the order in which she came into the world after her siblings.

It was only after she ran away, at seventeen, from her arranged marriage to a man three times her age, that Lan named herself. One night, she brewed her husband a pot of tea, dropping a pinch of lotus stems to deepen his sleep, then waited till the palm-leaf walls shivered with his snoring. Through the flat black night, she made her way, feeling one low branch after another.

Hours later, she knocked on the door to her mother's house. "Seven," her mother said through a crack in the door, "a girl who leaves her husband is the rot of a harvest. You know this. How can you not know?" And then the door closed, but not before a hand, gnarled as wood, pressed a pair of pearl earrings into

Lan's grip. The mother's pale face erased by the door's swing, the lock's click.

The crickets were too loud as Lan stumbled toward the nearest streetlamp, then followed each dim post, one by one, until, by dawn, the city appeared, smeared with fog.

A man selling rice cakes spotted her, her soiled nightgown torn at the collar, and offered a scoop of sweet rice steaming on a banana leaf. She dropped down in the dirt and chewed, eyes fixed on the ground between her coal-shaded feet.

"Where are you from," the man asked, "a young girl like you wandering at this hour? What is your name?"

Her mouth filled itself with that lush sound, the tone forming through the chewed rice before the vowel rose, its protracted ah, pronounced Laang. Orchid, she decided, for no reason. "Lan," she said, the rice falling, like chipped light, from her lips. "Tên tôi là Lan."

Surrounding the boy soldier, the woman, and the girl is the land's verdant insistence. But which land? Which border that was crossed and erased, divided and rearranged?

Twenty-eight now, she has given birth to a girl she wraps in a piece of sky stolen from a clear day.

Sometimes, at night, the girl asleep, Lan stares into the dark, thinking of another world, one where a woman holds her daughter by the side of a road, a thumbnail moon hung in the clear air. A world where there are no soldiers or Hueys and the woman is only going for a walk in the warm spring evening, where she speaks real soft to her daughter, telling her the story of a girl who ran away from her faceless youth only to name herself after a flower that opens like something torn apart.

Due to their ubiquity and diminutive size, macaques are the most hunted primates in Southeast Asia.

The white-haired man raises a glass and makes a toast, grins. Five other glasses are lifted to meet his, the light falls in each shot because the law says so. The shots are held by arms that belong to men who will soon cut open the macaque's skull with a scalpel, open it like a lid on a jar. The men will take turns consuming the brain, dipped in alcohol or swallowed with cloves of garlic from a porcelain plate, all while the monkey kicks beneath them. The fishing rod cast and cast but never hitting water. The men believe the meal will rid them of impotence, that the more the monkey rages, the stronger the cure. They are doing this for the future of their genes—for the sake of sons and daughters.

They wipe their mouths with napkins printed with sunflowers that soon grow brown, then start to tear—soaked.

After, at night, the men will come home renewed, their stomachs full, and press themselves against their wives and lovers. The scent of floral makeup—cheek to cheek.

A sound now of dribbling. A liquid warmth slides down the hem of her black trousers. The acrid smell of ammonia. Lan pisses herself in front of the two boys—and holds the girl tighter. Around her feet a circle of wet heat. The brain of the macaque monkey is the closest, of any mammal, to a human's.

The raindrops darken as they slide down the blond soldier's dirt-baked cheeks before collecting, like ellipses, along his jaw.

"Yoo Et Aye numbuh won," she says, urine still dripping down her ankles. Then again, louder. "Yoo Et Aye numbuh won. No bang bang." She raises her free hand to the sky, as if to let someone pull her right up to it. "No bang bang. Yoo Et Aye numbuh won."

A tic in the boy's left eye. A green leaf falling into a green pond.

He stares at the girl, her too-pink skin. The girl whose name is Hong, or Rose. Because why not another flower? Hong—a syllable the mouth must swallow whole at once. Orchid and Rose, side by side on this breath-white road. A mother holding a daughter. A rose growing out of the stem of an orchid.

He takes note of Rose's hair, its errant cinnamon tint fringed blond around the temples. Seeing the soldier's eyes on her daughter, Lan pushes the girl's face to her chest, shielding her. The boy watches this child, the whiteness showing from her yellow body. He could be her father, he thinks, realizes. Someone he knows could be her father—his sergeant, squad leader, platoon partner, Michael, George, Thomas, Raymond, Jackson. He considers them, rifle gripped tight, his eyes on the girl with American blood before the American gun.

"No bang bang . . . Yoo Et Aye . . . ," Lan whispers now. "Yoo Et Aye . . ."

Macaques are capable of self-doubt and introspection, traits once thought attributable only to humans. Some species have displayed behavior indicating the use of judgment, creativity, even language. They are able to recall past images and apply them to current problem solving. In other words, macaques employ memory in order to survive.

The men will eat until the animal is empty, the monkey slowing as they spoon, its limbs heavy and listless. When nothing's left, when all of its memories dissolve into the men's bloodstreams, the monkey dies. Another bottle will be opened.

Who will be lost in the story we tell ourselves? Who will be lost in ourselves? A story, after all, is a kind of swallowing. To open a mouth, in speech, is to leave only the bones, which remain untold. It is a beautiful country because you are still breathing.

Yoo Et Aye numbuh won. Hands up. Don't shoot. Yoo Et Aye numbuh won. Hands up. No bang bang.

The rain keeps on because nourishment, too, is a force. The first soldier steps back. The second one moves the wooden divider, waves the woman forward. The houses behind her now reduced to bonfires. As the Huey returns to the sky, the rice stalks erect themselves, only slightly disheveled. The shawl drenched indigo with sweat and rain.

In the garage, on a wall of stripped paint, spotted brick underneath, a shelf hangs as a makeshift altar. On it are framed pictures where saints, dictators, and martyrs, the dead—a mother and father—stare out, unblinking. In the glass frames, the reflection of sons leaning back in their chairs. One of them pours what's left of the bottle over the sticky table, wipes it clean. A white cloth is placed over the macaque's hollowed mind. The light in the garage flickers once, stays on.

The woman stands in a circle of her own piss. No, she is standing on the life-sized period of her own sentence, alive. The boy turns, walks back to his post at the checkpoint. The other boy taps his helmet and nods at her, his finger, she notices, still on the trigger. It is a beautiful country because you are still in it. Because your name is Rose, and you are my mother and the year is 1968— the Year of the Monkey.

The woman walks forward. Passing the guard, she glances one last time at the rifle. The muzzle, she notices, is not darker than her daughter's mouth. The light flickers once, stays on.

I wake to the sound of an animal in distress. The room so dark I can't tell if my eyes are even open. There's a breeze through the cracked window, and with it an August night, sweet but cut with the bleach smell of lawn chemicals—the scent of manicured suburban yards—and I realize I'm not in my own house.

I sit up on the side of the bed and listen. Maybe it's a cat wounded from a skirmish with a raccoon. I balance myself in the black air and head toward the hallway. There's a red blade of light coming through a cracked door at the other end. The animal is inside the house. I palm the wall, which, in the humidity, feels like wet skin. I make my way toward the door and hear, in between the whimpers, the animal's breaths—heavier now, something with huge lungs, much larger than a cat. I peer through the door's red crack—and that's when I see him: the man bent over in a reading chair, his white skin and even whiter hair made pink, raw under a scarlet-shaded lamp. And it comes to me: I'm in Virginia, on summer break. I'm nine. The man's name is Paul. He is my grandfather—and he's crying. A warped Polaroid trembles between his fingers.

I push the door. The red blade widens. He looks up at me, lost, this white man with watery eyes. There are no animals here but us.

Paul had met Lan in 1967 while stationed in Cam Ranh Bay with the US Navy. They met at a bar in Saigon, dated, fell in love, and, a year later, married right there in the city's central courthouse. All through my childhood their wedding photo hung on the living room wall. In it, a thin, boyish Virginian farmboy with doe-brown eyes, not yet twenty-three, beams above his new wife, five years his senior—a farmgirl, as it happens, from Go Cong, and a mother to twelve-year-old Mai from her arranged marriage. As I played with my dolls and toy soldiers, that photo hovered over me, an icon from an epicenter that would lead to my own life. In the couple's hopeful smiles, it's hard to imagine the photo was snapped during one of the most brutal years of the war. At the time it was taken, with Lan's hand on Paul's chest, her pearl wedding ring a bead of light, you were already a year old—waiting in a stroller a few feet behind the cameraman as the bulb flashed.

Lan told me one day, while I was plucking her white hairs, that when she first arrived in Saigon, after running away from her doomed first marriage, after failing to find a job, she ended up as a sex worker for American GIs on R&R. She said, with barbed pride, as if she was defending herself before a jury, "I did what any mother would do, I made a way to eat. Who can judge me, huh? Who?" Her chin jutted, her head lifted high at some invisible person across the room. It was only when I heard her slip that I realized she was, in fact, speaking to someone: her mother. "I never wanted to, Ma. I wanted to go home with you—" She lunged forward. The tweezers dropped from my grip, pinged on the hardwood. "I never asked to be a whore," she sobbed. "A girl who leaves her husband is the rot of a harvest," she repeated the proverb her mother told her. "A girl who leaves . . ." She rocked from side to side, eyes shut, face lifted toward the ceiling, like she was seventeen again.

At first I thought she was telling another one of her half-invented tales, but the details grew clearer as her voice stammered into focus on odd yet idiosyncratic moments in the narrative. How the soldiers would smell of a mixture of tar, smoke, and mint Chiclets—the scent of the battle sucked so deep into their flesh it would linger even after their rigorous showers. Leaving Mai in the care of her sister back in the village, Lan rented a windowless room from a fisherman by the river, where she took the soldiers. How the fisherman, living below her, would spy on her through a slot in the wall. How the soldiers' boots were so heavy, when they kicked them off as they climbed into bed, the thumps sounded like bodies dropping, making her flinch under their searching hands.

Lan tensed as she spoke, her tone strained as it dipped into the realm of her second mind. She turned to me afterward, a finger blurred over her lips. "Shhhh. Don't tell your mom." Then she gave my nose a flick, her eyes bright as she grinned maniacally.

But Paul, shy and sheepish, who often spoke with his hands in his lap, was not her client—which was why they hit it off. According to Lan, they did, in fact, meet at a bar. It was late, nearly midnight, when Lan walked in. She had just finished her work for the day and was getting a nightcap when she saw the "lost boy," as she called him, sitting alone at the counter. There was a social that night for servicemen in one of the ritzy hotels, and Paul was waiting for a date that would never arrive.

They talked over drinks and found a common ground in their shared rural childhoods, both having been brought up in the "sticks" of their respective countries. These two unlikely hillbillies must have found a familiar dialect that fused the gap between their estranged vernaculars. Despite their vastly different paths, they found themselves transplants in a decadent and disorientating city besieged by bombing raids. It was in this familiar happenstance that they found refuge in each other.

One night, two months after they met, Lan and Paul would be holed up in a one-room apartment in Saigon. The city was being infiltrated by a massive North Vietnamese advance that would later be known as the infamous Tet Offensive. All night Lan lay fetal, her back against the wall, Paul by her side, his standard-issue 9mm pistol aimed at the door as the city tore open with sirens and mortar fire.

Although it's only three in the morning, the lampshade makes the room feel like the last moments of a sinister sunset. Under the bulb's electric hum, Paul and I spot each other through the doorway. He wipes his eyes with the palm of one hand and waves me over with the other. He slips the photo into his chest pocket and puts on his glasses, blinking hard. I sit on the cherrywood arm-chair beside him.

"You okay, Grandpa?" I say, still foggy from sleep. His smile has a grimace underneath it. I suggest that I go back to bed, that it's still early anyway, but he shakes his head.

"It's alright." He sniffles and straightens up in the chair, seri-ous. "It's just—well, I just keep thinking about that song you sang earlier, the uh . . ." He squints at the floor.

"Ca trù," I offer, "the folk songs—the ones Grandma used to sing."

"That's right." He nods vigorously. "Ca trù. I was lying there in the damn dark and I swear I kept hearing it. It's been so long since I heard that sound." He glances at me, searching, then back at the floor. "I must be going crazy."

Earlier that night, after dinner, I had sung a few folk songs for Paul. He had inquired about what I had learned during the school year and, already steeped in summer and drawing a blank, I of-fered a few songs I had memorized from Lan. I sang, in my best effort, a classic lullaby Lan used to sing. The song, originally per-formed by the famous Khánh Ly, describes a woman singing among corpses strewn across sloping leafy hills. Searching the faces of the dead, the singer asks in the song's refrain, *And which of you, which of you are my sister?*

Do you remember it, Ma, how Lan would sing it out of nowhere? How once, she sang it at my friend Junior's birthday party, her face the shade of raw ground beef from a single Heineken? You shook her shoulder, telling her to stop, but she kept going, eyes closed, swaying side to side as she sang. Junior and his family didn't understand Vietnamese—thank god. To them it was just my crazy grandma mumbling away again. But you and I could hear it. Eventually you put down your slice of pineapple cake—untouched, the glasses clinking as the corpses, fleshed from Lan's mouth, piled up around us.

Among the empty plates stained from the baked ziti, I sang that same song as Paul listened. After, he simply clapped, then we washed up. I had forgotten that Paul, too, understands Vietnamese, having picked it up during the war.

"I'm sorry," I say now, watching the red light pool under his eyes. "It's a stupid song anyway."

Outside, the wind is driving through the maples, their rinsed leaves slap against the clapboard siding. "Let's just make some coffee or something, Grandpa."

"Right." He pauses, mulling something over, then rises to his feet. "Let me just put on my slippers. I'm always cold in the mornings. I swear something's wrong with me. It's getting old. Your body heat retreats to your center until one day your feet are ice." He almost laughs but rubs his chin instead, then raises his arm, as if to strike at something in front of him—and then the click, the lamp goes out, the room now swept with a violet stillness. From the shadow, his voice: "I'm glad you're here, Little Dog."

"Why do they say black?" you asked weeks earlier, back in Hartford, pointing to Tiger Woods on the TV screen. You squinted at the white ball on the tee. "His mom is Taiwanese, I've seen her face, but they always say black. Shouldn't they at least say half yellow?" You folded your bag of Doritos, tucked it under your arm. "How come?" You tilted your head, waiting for my answer.

When I said that I didn't know, you raised your eyebrows. "What do you mean?" You grabbed the controller and turned up the volume. "Listen closely, and tell us why this man is not Taiwanese," you said, running your hand through your hair. Your eyes followed Woods as he walked back and forth across the screen, periodically crouching to gauge his stroke. There was no mention, at the moment, of his ethnic makeup, and the answer you wanted never came. You stretched a strand of hair before your face, examining it. "I need to get more curlers."

Lan, who was sitting on the floor beside us, said, without looking up from the apple she was peeling, "That boy don't look Taiwanese to me. He looks Puerto Rican."

You gave me a look, leaned back, and sighed. "Everything good is always somewhere else," you said after a while, and changed the channel.

When we arrived in America in 1990, color was one of the first things we knew of yet knew nothing about. Once we stepped inside our one-bedroom apartment in the predominantly Latinx neighborhood on Franklin Avenue that winter, the rules of color, and with it our faces, had changed. Lan, who, back in Vietnam, was considered dark, was now lighter. And you, Ma—so fair you would "pass" for white, like the time we were in the Sears department store and the blond clerk, bending down to stroke my hair, asked you whether I was "yours or adopted." Only when you stuttered, your English garbled, gone, head lowered, did she realize her mistake. Even when you looked the part, your tongue outed you.

One does not "pass" in America, it seems, without English.

"No, madam," I said to the woman in my ESL English. "That's my mom. I came out her asshole and I love her very much. I am seven. Next year I will be eight. I'm doing fine. I feel good how about you? Merry Christmas Happy New Year." The deluge was exactly eighty percent of the language I knew at the time and I shivered in pure delight as the words flew out of me.

You believed, like many Vietnamese mothers, that to speak of female genitalia, especially between mothers and sons, is considered taboo—so when talking about birth, you always mentioned that I had come out of your anus. You would playfully slap my head and say, "This huge noggin nearly tore up my asshole!"

Startled, her perm throbbing, the clerk turned and clacked away on her heels. You looked down at me. "What the hell did you say?"

In 1966, in between his two tours in Vietnam, Earl Dennison Woods, a lieutenant colonel in the United States Army, was stationed in Thailand. There, he met Kultida Punsawad, a Thai native and secretary for the US Army office in Bangkok. After dating for a year, Earl and Kultida moved to Brooklyn, New York, where, in 1969, they got married. Earl would return to Vietnam for one final tour, from 1970 to 1971, right before American involvement in the conflict began to decline. By the time Saigon fell, Earl officially retired from military service to begin his new life, and most important, raise his new son—born only six months after the last US helicopter lifted from the American embassy in Saigon.

The boy's birth name, according to an ESPN profile I read a while back, was Eldrick Tont Woods. His first name a unique formulation of the E in "Earl" and ending in the K in "Kultida." His parents, whose home in Brooklyn was often vandalized due to their interracial marriage, decided to stand at each end of their son's name, like pillars. Eldrick's middle name, Tont, is a traditional Thai name given to him by his mother. However, shortly after his birth, the boy obtained a nickname that would soon become famous across the globe.

Eldrick "Tiger" Woods, one of the greatest golfers in the world is, like you, Ma, a direct product of the war in Vietnam.

Paul and I are in his garden harvesting fresh basil for a pesto recipe he promised to teach me. We successfully avoid talking about the past, having brushed by it earlier that morning. We talk, instead, of cage-free eggs. He pauses from his picking, pulls his cap over his brow and lectures, with steeled intensity, on how antibiotics cause infections in commercially farmed hens, that the bees are dying and how, without them, the country would lose its entire food supply in less than three months, how you should cook olive oil on low heat because burning it would release free radicals that cause cancer.

We sidestep ourselves in order to move forward.

In the next yard, a neighbor starts up his leaf blower. The leaves flutter and land in the street with a series of little clicks. When Paul bends to tug at a braid of ragweed, the photo in his pocket falls out, landing faceup on the grass. A black-and-white Polaroid, slightly larger than a box of matches, it shows a group of young people with faces smeared by laughter. Despite Paul's quickness— sticking it back in his pocket soon as it lands—I make out the two faces I know too well: Paul and Lan, their arms around each other, eyes burning with an exuberance so rare it looks fake.

In the kitchen, Paul pours me a bowl of Raisin Bran with water—just how I like it. He plops down at the table, takes off his cap, and reaches for one of the already rolled joints lined, like thin sticks of packaged sugar, inside a porcelain teacup. Three years ago, Paul was diagnosed with cancer, something he believed was brought on by his contact with Agent Orange during his tour. The tumor was on the nape of his neck, right above the spinal cord. Luckily, the doctors caught it before it invaded his brain. After a year of failed chemotherapy, they decided to operate. The whole process, from diagnosis to remission, took nearly two years.

Leaning back now in his chair, Paul cups a flame in his palm and pulls it through the joint's length. He sucks, the tip intensifying as I watch. He smokes the way one smokes after a funeral. On the kitchen wall behind him are colored-pencil drawings of Civil War generals I had made for a school project. You had sent them to Paul months earlier. The smoke blows across the primary-colored profile of Stonewall Jackson, then fades.

Before bringing me to Paul's, you sat me down on your bed back in Hartford, took a long drag on your cigarette, and just said it.

"Listen. No, look at me right here, I'm serious. Listen." You put both hands on my shoulder, the smoke thickening around us. "He's not your grandfather. Okay?"

The words entered me as if through a vein.

"Which means he's not my father either. Got it? Look at me." When you're nine, you know when to shut your mouth, so I did, thinking you were only upset, that all daughters must say this, at some point, of their fathers. But you kept going, your voice calm and cool, like stones being laid, one by one, upon a long wall. You said that when Lan met Paul that night in the bar in Saigon, Lan was already four months pregnant. The father, the real one, was just another American john—faceless, nameless, less. Except for you. All that remains of him is you, is me. "Your grandfather is nobody." You sat back, the cigarette returned to your lips.

Up to that point I thought I had, if nothing else, a tether to this country, a grandfather, one with a face, an identity, a man who could read and write, one who called me on my birthdays, whom I was a part of, whose American name ran inside my blood. Now that cord was cut. Your face and hair a mess, you got up to flick the Marlboro into the sink. "Everything good is somewhere else, baby. I'm telling you. Everything."

Leaning into the table now, the photo safely tucked in his shirt pocket, Paul starts to tell me what I already know. "Hey," he says, eyes glazed with reefer. "I'm not who I am. I mean . . ." He dabs the joint into his half-full glass of water. It hisses. My Raisin Bran, untouched, crackles in its red clay bowl. "I'm not what your mamma says I am." His gaze is lowered as he tells it, his rhythm cut with odd pauses, at times slipping into near-whisper, like a man cleaning his rifle at daybreak and talking to himself. And I let him run his mind. I let him empty. I didn't stop him because you don't stop nothing when you're nine.

One evening, during his final tour in Vietnam, Earl Woods found himself pinned down by enemy fire. The American fire base he was stationed at was about to be overrun by a large North Vietnamese and Viet Cong contingent. Most of the American GIs had already evacuated. Woods was not alone—beside him, hunkered down in their two-jeep caravan, was Lieutenant Colonel Vuong Dang Phong. Phong, as Woods described him, was a ferocious pilot and commander, with a ruthless eye for detail. He was also a dear friend. As the enemy poured in around the abandoned base, Phong turned to Woods, assuring him they'll live through it.

For the next four hours, the two friends sat in their jeeps, their olive uniforms darkened with sweat. Woods clutched his M-79 grenade launcher as Phong held the jeeps' machine-gun turret. In this way, they survived the night. After, the two would share a drink in Phong's room back at base camp—and laugh, discussing baseball, jazz, and philosophy.

All through his time in Vietnam, Phong was Woods's confidant. Perhaps such strong bonds are inevitable between men who trust each other with their lives. Perhaps it was their mutual otherness that drew them close, Woods being both black and Native American, growing up in the segregated American South, and Phong, a sworn enemy to half of his countrymen in an army run, at its core, by white American generals. Whatever the case, before Woods left Vietnam, the two swore to find each other after the helicopters, bombers, and napalm had lifted. Neither of them knew it would be the last time they saw each other.

Being a high-ranking colonel, Phong was captured by the North Vietnamese authorities thirty-nine days after Saigon was taken. He was sent to a reeducation camp where he was tortured, starved, and committed to forced labor.

A year later, at age forty-seven, Phong died while in detainment. His grave would not be discovered until a decade later, when his children unearthed his bones for reburial near his home province—the final gravestone reading *Vuong Dung Phong.*

But to Earl Woods, his friend was known as none other than "Tiger Phong"—or simply Tiger, a nickname Woods had given him for his ferocity in battle.

On December 30, 1975, a year before Tiger Phong's death and across the world from Phong's jail cell, Earl was in Cypress, California, cradling a newborn boy in his arms. The boy already had the name Eldrick but, staring into the infant's eyes, Earl knew the boy would have to be named after his best friend, Tiger. "Someday, my old friend would see him on television . . . and say, 'That must be Woody's kid,' and we'd find each other again," Earl later said in an interview.

Tiger Phong died of heart failure, most likely brought on by poor nutrition and exhaustion at the camp. But for a brief eight months in 1975 and 1976, the two most important Tigers in Earl Woods's life were alive at once, sharing the same planet, one at the fragile end of a brutal history, the other just beginning a legacy of his own. The name "Tiger," but also Earl himself, had become a bridge.

When Earl finally heard news of Tiger Phong's death, Tiger Woods had already won his first Masters. "Boy, does this ever hurt," Earl said. "I've got that old feeling in my stomach, that combat feeling."

I remember the day you went to your first church service. Junior's dad was a light-skinned Dominican, his ma a black Cuban, and they worshipped at the Baptist church on Prospect Ave., where no one asked them why they rolled their r's or where they *really* came from. I had already gone to the church with the Ramirezes a handful of times, when I'd sleep over on Saturday and wake up attending services in Junior's borrowed Sunday best. That day, after being invited by Dionne, you decided to go—out of politeness but also because the church gave out nearly expired groceries donated by local supermarkets.

You and I were the only yellow faces in the church. But when Dionne and Miguel introduced us to their friends, we were received with warm smiles. "Welcome to my father's house," people kept saying. And I remember wondering how so many people could be related, could all come from the same dad.

I was enamored of the verve, torque, and tone of the pastor's voice, his sermon on Noah's Ark inflected with hesitations, rhetorical questions amplified by long silences that intensified the story's effect. I loved the way the pastor's hands moved, flowed, as if his sentences had to be shaken off him in order to reach us. It was, to me, a new kind of embodiment, one akin to magic, one I'd glimpsed only partially in Lan's own storytelling.

But that day, it was the *song* that offered me a new angle of seeing the world, which is to say, seeing you. Once the piano and organ roared into the first thick chords of "His Eye Is on the Sparrow," everyone in the congregation rose, shuffling, and let their arms fly out above them, some turning in circles. Hundreds of boots and heels hammered the wooden floors. In the blurred gyrations, the twirling coats and scarfs, I felt a pinch on my wrist. Your fingernails were white as they dug into my skin. Your face—eyes closed—lifted toward the ceiling, you were saying something to the fresco of angels above us.

At first I couldn't hear through the sound of clapping and shouting. It was all a kaleidoscope of color and movement as fat organ and trumpet notes boomed through the pews from the brass band. I wrested my arm from your grip. When I leaned in, I heard your words underneath the song—you were speaking to your father. Your real one. Cheeks wet with tears, you nearly shouted. "Where are you, Ba?" you demanded in Vietnamese, shifting from foot to foot. "Where the hell are you? Come get me! Get me out of here! Come back and get me." It might have been the first time Vietnamese was ever spoken in that church. But no one glared at you with questions in their eyes. No one made a double take at the yellow-white woman speaking her own tongue. Throughout the pews other people were also shouting, in excitement, joy, anger, or exasperation. It was there, inside the song, that you had permission to lose yourself and not be wrong.

I stared at the toddler-sized plaster of Jesus hanging to the side of the pulpit. His skin seemed to throb from the stamping feet. He was regarding his petrified toes with an expression of fatigued bewilderment, as if he had just woken from a deep sleep only to find himself nailed red and forever to this world. I studied him for so long that when I turned to your white sneakers I half expected a pool of blood under your feet.

Days later, I would hear "His Eye Is on the Sparrow" coming from the kitchen. You were at the table, practicing your manicurist techniques on rubber mannequin hands. Dionne had given you a tape of gospel songs, and you hummed along as you worked, as the disembodied hands, their fingers lustered with candy colors, sprouted along the kitchen counters, their palms open, like the ones back in that church. But unlike the darker hands in the Ramirezes' congregation, the ones in your kitchen were pink and beige, the only shades they came in.

1964: When commencing his mass bombing campaign in North Vietnam, General Curtis LeMay, then chief of staff of the US Air Force, said he planned on bombing the Vietnamese "back into the Stone Ages." To destroy a people, then, is to set them back in time. The US military would end up releasing over ten thousand tons of bombs in a country no larger than the size of California— surpassing the number of bombs deployed in all of WWII combined.

1997: Tiger Woods wins the Masters Tournament, his first major championship in professional golf.

1998: Vietnam opens its first professional golf course, which was designed on a rice paddy formerly bombed by the US Air Force. One of the playing holes was made by filling in a bomb crater.

Paul finishes his portion of the story. And I want to tell him. I want to say that his daughter who is not his daughter was a half-white child in Go Cong, which meant the children called her ghost-girl, called Lan a traitor and a whore for sleeping with the enemy. How they cut her auburn-tinted hair while she walked home from the market, arms full with baskets of bananas and green squash, so that when she got home, there'd be only a few locks left above her forehead. How when she ran out of hair, they slapped buffalo shit on her face and shoulders to make her *brown again,* as if to be born lighter was a wrong that could be reversed. Maybe this is why, I realize now, it mattered to you what they called Tiger Woods on TV, how you needed color to be a fixed and inviolable fact.

"Maybe you shouldn't call me Grandpa anymore." Paul's cheeks pinch as he sucks the second joint, killing it. He looks like a fish. "That word, it might be a bit awkward now wouldn't it?"

I think about it for a minute. Ulysses Grant's Crayola portrait quivers from a breeze through the dimming window.

"No," I say after a while, "I don't got any other grandpa. So I wanna keep calling you that."

He nods, resigned, his pale forehead and white hair tinted with evening light. "Of course. Of course," he says as the roach drops into the glass with a sizzle, leaving a thread of smoke that twirls, like a ghostly vein, up his arms. I stare at the brown mash in the bowl before me, now soggy.

There is so much I want to tell you, Ma. I was once foolish enough to believe knowledge would clarify, but some things are so gauzed behind layers of syntax and semantics, behind days and hours, names forgotten, salvaged and shed, that simply knowing the wound exists does nothing to reveal it.

I don't know what I'm saying. I guess what I mean is that sometimes I don't know what or who we are. Days I feel like a human being, while other days I feel more like a sound. I touch the world not as myself but as an echo of who I was. Can you hear me yet? Can you read me?

When I first started writing, I hated myself for being so uncertain, about images, clauses, ideas, even the pen or journal I used. Everything I wrote began with *maybe* and *perhaps* and ended with *I think* or *I believe*. But my doubt is everywhere, Ma. Even when I know something to be true as bone I fear the knowledge will dissolve, will not, despite my writing it, stay real. I'm breaking us apart again so that I might carry us somewhere else—where, exactly, I'm not sure. Just as I don't know what to call you—White, Asian, orphan, American, mother?

Sometimes we are given only two choices. While doing research, I read an article from an 1884 El Paso *Daily Times,* which reported that a white railroad worker was on trial for the murder of an unnamed Chinese man. The case was ultimately dismissed.

The judge, Roy Bean, cited that Texas law, while prohibiting the murder of human beings, defined a human only as White, African American, or Mexican. The nameless yellow body was not considered human because it did not fit in a slot on a piece of paper. Sometimes you are erased before you are given the choice of stating who you are.

To be or not to be. That is the question.

When you were a girl in Vietnam, the neighborhood kids would take a spoon to your arms, shouting, "Get the white off her, get the white off her!" Eventually you learned to swim. Wading deep into the muddy river, where no one could reach you, no one could scrape you away. You made yourself an island for hours at a time. Coming home, your jaw would clatter from cold, your arms pruned and blistered—but still white.

When asked how he identifies his roots, Tiger Woods called himself "Cablinasian," a portmanteau he invented to contain his ethnic makeup of Chinese, Thai, Black, Dutch, and Native American.

To be or not to be. That is the question. A question, yes, but not a choice.

"I remember one time, while visiting you all in Hartford—this must be a year or two after you landed from Vietnam—" Paul rests his chin on his palm and stares out the window, where a hummingbird hovers at the plastic feeder. "I walked into the apartment and found you crying under the table. No one was home—or maybe your mom was—but she must have been in the bathroom or something." He stops, letting the memory fill in. "I bent down and asked you what was wrong, and you know what you said?" He grins. "You said that the other kids lived more than you. What a hoot." He shakes his head. "What a thing to say! I'll never forget that." His gold-capped molar caught the light. "'They live more, they live more!' you shouted. Who the hell gave you that idea? You were only five, for Christ sakes."

Outside, the hummingbird's whirring sounds almost like human breath. Its beak jabs into the pool of sugared water at the feeder's base. What a terrible life, I think now, to have to move so fast just to stay in one place.

After, we go for a walk, Paul's brown-spotted beagle clinking between us. It's just after sunset and the air's thick with sweetgrass and late lilacs frothing white and magenta along the manicured lawns. We veer toward the last bend when a plain-looking lady, middle-aged, hair in a blond ponytail, approaches. She says, looking only at Paul, "I see you finally got a dog boy. Good for you, Paul!"

Paul stops, pushes his glasses up his nose only to have them slide back down. She turns to me, articulates, "Welcome. To. The. Neighbor. Hood." Her head bobs out each syllable.

I hold tight the dog's leash and step back, offering a smile.

"No," Paul says, his hand raised awkwardly, as if waving away cobwebs. "This is my grandson." He lets the word hover between us all, until it feels solid, an instrument, then repeats it, nodding, to himself or the woman I can't say. "My grandson."

Without a beat the woman smiles. Too widely.

"Please remember that."

She laughs, makes a dismissive gesture before extending her hand to me, my body now legible.

I let her shake my hand.

"Well, I'm Carol. Welcome to the neighborhood. I mean that." She walks on.

We head home. We don't speak. Behind the row of white town houses, a column of spruces stands motionless against a reddish sky. The beagle's paws scrape the concrete, its chain clinking as the animal pulls us home. But all I can hear is Paul's voice in my head. *My grandson. This is my grandson.*

I'm dragged into a hole, darker than the night around it, by two women. Only when one of them screams do I know who I am. I see their heads, black hair matted from the floor they sleep on. The air sharp with a chemical delirium as they jostle in the blur of the car's interior. Eyes still thick with sleep, I make out the shapes: a headrest, a felt monkey the size of a thumb swinging from the rearview, a piece of metal, shining, then gone. The car peels out of the driveway, and I can tell, from the smell of acetone and nail polish, that it's your tan-and-rust Toyota. You and Lan are in the front, clamoring for something that won't show itself. The streetlights fling by, hitting your faces with the force of blows.

"He's gonna kill her, Ma. He's gonna do it this time," you say, breathless.

"We riding. We riding helicopter fast." Lan is in her own mind, red and dense with obsession. "We riding where?" She clutches the flip-down mirror with both hands. I can tell by her voice that she is smiling, or at least gritting her teeth.

"He's gonna kill my sister, Mama." You sound like you're flailing down a river. "I know Carl. It's for real this time. You hear me? Ma!"

Lan rocks side to side from the mirror, making whooshing sounds. "We getting out of here, huh? We gotta go far, Little Dog!" Outside, the night surges by like sideways gravity. The green numbers on the dash read 3:04. Who put my hands in my face? The tires squeal at each turn. The streets are empty and it feels like a universe in here, an *everything* hurling through the cosmic dark while, in the front seat, the women who raised me are losing their minds. Through my fingers, the night is black construction paper. Only the frazzled heads of these two before me are clear, swaying.

"Don't worry, Mai." You're speaking to yourself now. Your face so close to the windshield the glass fogs a ring that spreads in equal measure to your words. "I'm coming. We're coming."

After a while we swerve down a street lined with Continentals. The car crawls, then stops in front of a grey clapboard town house. "Mai," you say, pulling the emergency brake. "He's gonna kill Mai."

Lan, who all this time had been shaking her head from side to side, stops, as if the words have finally touched a little button inside her. "What? Who kill who? Who die this time?"

"Both of you stay in the car!" You unbuckle your belt, leap out, and shuffle toward the house, the door left open behind you.

There's a story Lan would tell, of Lady Triệu, the mythical woman warrior who led an army of men and repelled the Chinese invasion of ancient Vietnam. I think of her, seeing you. How, as legend goes, armed with two swords, she'd fling her yard-long breasts over her shoulders and cut down the invaders by the dozens. How it was a woman who saved us.

"Who die now?" Lan swings around, her face, made stark by the overhead light, ripples with this new knowledge. "Who gonna die, Little Dog?" She flips her hand back and forth, as if opening a locked door, to indicate emptiness. "Somebody kill you? For what?"

But I'm not listening. I'm rolling down the window, arms burning with each turn on the handle. Cool November air slips in. My stomach grabs as I watch you mount the front steps, the nine-inch machete glinting in your hand. You knock on the door, shouting. "Come out, Carl," you say in Vietnamese. "Come out, you fucker! I'm taking her home for good. You can have the car, just give me my sister." At the word *sister* your voice cracks into a short, busted sob, before regaining control. You bash the door with the machete's wooden butt.

The porch lights turn on, your pink nightgown suddenly green under the fluorescent. The door opens.

You step back.

A man appears. He half lunges from the doorway as you backpedal down the steps. The blade locked at your side, as if pinned in place.

"He has a gun," Lan whisper-shouts from the car, now lucid. "Rose! It's a shotgun. It shoots two eaters at once. They eat your lungs inside out. Little Dog, tell her."

Your hands float over your head, the metal clanks on the driveway. The man, huge, his shoulders sloped under a grey Yankees sweatshirt, steps up to you, says a few words through his teeth, then kicks the machete to the side. It disappears in the grass with a flash. You mumble something, make yourself small, cup your hands under your chin, the posture you take after receiving a tip at the salon. The man lowers his gun as you back away, shaking, toward the car.

"It's not worth it, Rose," Lan says, cupping her mouth with both hands. "You can't beat a gun. You just can't. Come back, come back in the helicopter."

"Ma," I hear myself say, my voice cracking. "Ma, come on."

You edge slowly into the driver's seat, turn to me with a nauseated stare. There's a long silence. I think you're about to laugh, but then your eyes fill. So I turn away, to the man carefully eyeing us, hand on his hip, the gun clamped between his armpit, pointed at the ground, protecting his family.

When you start to talk, your voice is scraped out. I catch only parts of it. It's not Mai's house, you explain, fumbling with your keys. Or rather, Mai is no longer there. The boyfriend, Carl, who used to slam her head against the wall is no longer there. This is somebody else, white man with a shotgun and a bald head. It was a mistake, you're saying to Lan. An accident.

"But Mai has not lived here for five years," Lan says with sudden tenderness. "Rose . . ." Although I don't see it, I can tell she's brushing your hair behind your ear. "Mai moved to Florida, remember? To open her own salon." Lan is poised, her shoulders relaxed, someone else has stepped inside her and started moving her limbs, her lips. "We go home. You need sleep, Rose."

The engine starts, the car lurches into a U-turn. As we pull away, from the porch, a boy, no older than I am, points a toy pistol at us. The gun jumps and his mouth makes blasting noises. His father turns to yell at him. He shoots once, two more times. From the window of my helicopter, I look at him. I look him dead in the eyes and do what you do. I refuse to die.

II

Memory is a choice. You said that once, with your back to me, the way a god would say it. But if you were a god you would see them. You would look down at this grove of pines, the fresh tips flared lucent at each treetop, tender-damp in their late autumn flush. You would look past the branches, past the rusted light splintered through the brambles, the needles falling, one by one, as you lay your god eyes on them. You'd trace the needles as they hurled themselves past the lowest bough, toward the cooling forest floor, to land on the two boys lying side by side, the blood already dry on their cheeks.

Although it covers both their faces, the blood belongs to the tall boy, the one with eyes the dark grey of a river beneath somebody's shadow. What's left of November seeps through their jeans, their thin knit sweaters. If you were god, you'd notice that they're staring up at you. They're clapping and singing "This Little Light of Mine," the Ralph Stanley version they'd listened to earlier in the afternoon on the tall boy's stereo. It was his old man's favorite song, the tall boy had said. And so now their heads sway side to side as their teeth glow between the notes, and the caked blood crumbles from their jaws, flecking their pale throats as the song leaves them in fistfuls of smoke. *"This little light of mine, I'm gonna let it shine. This little light of mine, I'm gonna let it shine.... All in my house, I'm gonna let it shine."* The pine needles spin and sputter around them in the minuscule wind made by their moving limbs. The cut under the tall boy's eye has reopened from his singing, and a black-red line now runs down his left ear, curving at his neck and vanishing in the ground. The small boy glances at his friend, the terrible bulb of an eye, and tries to forget.

If you were god you would tell them to stop clapping. You would tell them that the most useful thing one can do with empty hands is hold on. But you are not a god.

You're a woman. A mother, and your son is lying under the pines while you sit at a kitchen table across town, waiting again. You have just reheated, for the third time, the pan of fried flat noodles and scallions. Your breath fogs the glass as you stare out the window, waiting for the boy's orange New York Knicks sweater to flash by, as he must be running, it being so late.

But your son is still under the trees beside the boy you will never meet. They are yards from the closed overpass, where a plastic bag thrashes against the chain link surrounded by hundreds of one-shot liquor bottles. The boys begin to shiver, their claps slow, nearly inaudible. Their voices subdued as the wind swarms hugely above them—needles clicking down like the hands of smashed watches.

There are times, late at night, when your son would wake believing a bullet is lodged inside him. He'd feel it floating on the right side of his chest, just between the ribs. *The bullet was always here,* the boy thinks, older even than himself—and his bones, tendons, and veins had merely wrapped around the metal shard, sealing it inside him. *It wasn't me,* the boy thinks, *who was inside my mother's womb, but this bullet, this seed I bloomed around.* Even now, as the cold creeps in around him, he feels it poking out from his chest, slightly tenting his sweater. He feels for the protrusion but, as usual, finds nothing. *It's receded,* he thinks. *It wants to stay inside me. It is nothing without me.* Because a bullet without a body is a song without ears.

Across town, facing the window, you consider reheating the noodles one more time. You sweep into your palm pieces of the paper napkin you had torn up, then get up to toss it out. You return to the chair, wait. That window, the same one your son had stopped at one night before coming in, the square of light falling across him as he watched your face, peering out at him. Evening had turned the glass into a mirror and you couldn't see him there, only the lines scored across your cheeks and brow, a face somehow ravaged by stillness. The boy, he watches his mother watch nothing, his entire self inside the phantom oval of her face, invisible.

The song long over, the cold a numbing sheath over their nerves. Under their clothes, goose bumps appear, making their thin, translucent hair rise, then bend against the fabric under their shirts.

"Hey Trev," your son says, his friend's blood crusted tight on his cheek. "Tell me a secret." Wind, pine needles, seconds.

"What kind?"

"Just—like . . . a normal secret. It doesn't have to suck."

"A normal one." The hush of thinking, steady breaths. The stars above them a vast smudge on a hastily-wiped chalkboard. "Can you go first?"

On the table across town, your fingers stop drumming the Formica.

"Okay. You ready?"

"Yeah."

You push back your chair, grab your keys, and walk out the door.

"I'm not scared of dying anymore."

(A pause, then laughter.)

The cold, like river water, rises to their throats.

Ma. You once told me that memory is a choice. But if you were god, you'd know it's a flood.

B ecause I am your son, what I know of work I know equally of loss. And what I know of both I know of your hands. Their once supple contours I've never felt, the palms already callused and blistered long before I was born, then ruined further from three decades in factories and nail salons. Your hands are hideous—and I hate everything that made them that way. I hate how they are the wreck and reckoning of a dream. How you'd come home, night after night, plop down on the couch, and fall asleep inside a minute. I'd come back with your glass of water and you'd already be snoring, your hands in your lap like two partially scaled fish.

What I know is that the nail salon is more than a place of work and workshop for beauty, it is also a place where our children are raised—a number of whom, like cousin Victor, will get asthma from years of breathing the noxious fumes into their still-developing lungs. The salon is also a kitchen where, in the back rooms, our women squat on the floor over huge woks that pop and sizzle over electric burners, cauldrons of phở simmer and steam up the cramped spaces with aromas of cloves, cinnamon, ginger, mint, and cardamom mixing with formaldehyde, toluene, acetone, Pine-Sol, and bleach. A place where folklore, rumors, tall tales, and jokes from the old country are told, expanded, laughter erupting in back rooms the size of rich people's closets, then quickly lulled into an eerie, untouched quiet. It's a makeshift classroom where we arrive, fresh off the boat, the plane, the depths, hoping the salon would be a temporary stop—until we get on our feet, or rather, until our jaws soften around English syllables—bend over workbooks at manicure desks, finishing homework for nighttime ESL classes that cost a quarter of our wages.

I won't stay here long, we might say. *I'll get a real job soon.* But more often than not, sometimes within months, even weeks, we will walk back into the shop, heads lowered, our manicure drills inside paper bags tucked under our arms, and ask for our jobs back. And often the owner, out of pity or understanding or both, will simply nod at an empty desk—for there is always an empty desk. Because no one stays long enough and someone is always just-gone. Because there are no salaries, health care, or contracts, the body being the only material to work with and work from. Having nothing, it becomes its own contract, a testimony of presence. We will do this for decades—until our lungs can no longer breathe without swelling, our livers hardening with chemicals— our joints brittle and inflamed from arthritis—stringing together a kind of life. A new immigrant, within two years, will come to know that the salon is, in the end, a place where dreams become the calcified knowledge of what it means to be awake in American bones—with or without citizenship—aching, toxic, and underpaid.

I hate and love your battered hands for what they can never be.

It's Sunday. I am ten. You open the salon door and the acetone from yesterday's manicures immediately stings my nostrils. But our noses soon adjust, like they always do. You don't own the salon, but it's your task to run it each Sunday—the slowest day of the week. Inside, you switch on the lights, plug in the automated pedicure chairs, the water gurgling through pipes under the seats as I head to the breakroom to make instant coffee.

You say my name without glancing up and I know to walk over to the door, unlock it, flip the *Open* sign back out to the street.

That's when I see her. About seventy, her hair white and windblown across a narrow face with mined-out blue eyes, she has the stare of someone who had gone beyond where she needed to go but kept walking anyway. She peers into the shop, clutching a burgandy alligator purse with both hands. I open the door and she steps inside, hobbling a bit. The wind had blown her olive scarf off her neck, and it now hangs on one shoulder, brushing the floor. You stand, smile. "How I hep you?" you ask in English.

"A pedicure, please." Her voice is thin, as if cut with static. I help her out of her coat, hang it on the rack, and lead her to the pedicure chair as you run the air jets in the foot tub, fill the bubbling water with salts and solvents. The scent of synthetic lavender fills the room. I hold her arm and help her onto the seat.

She smells of dried sweat mixed with the strong sweetness of drug-store perfume. Her wrist throbs in my grip as she lowers herself into the seat. She seems even frailer than she looks. Once she eases back in the leather chair, she turns to me. I can't hear her over the water jets but can tell by her lips that she's saying, "Thank you."

When the jets are done, the water warm, an emerald green marbled with white suds, you ask her to lower her feet into the tub.

She won't budge. Her eyes closed.

"Ma'am," you say. The salon, usually bustling with people or music or the TV with Oprah or the news, is now silent. Only the lights hum above us. After a moment, she opens her eyes, the blue ringed pink and wet, and bends over to fiddle with her right pant leg. I take a step back. Your stool creaks as you shift your weight, your gaze fixed on her fingers. The pale veins on her hands shiver as she rolls up her pant leg. The skin is glossy, as if dipped in a kiln. She reaches lower, grabs her ankle, and, with a jerk, detaches her entire lower leg at the knee.

A prosthesis.

Halfway down her shinbone, a brownish stub protrudes, smooth and round as the end of a baguette—or what it is, an amputated leg. I glance at you, hoping for an answer. Without skipping a beat, you take out your file and start to scrub her one foot, the puckered nub beside it shaking from the work. The woman places the prosthesis at her side, her arm resting protec-tively around its calf, then sits back, exhaling. "Thank you," she says again, louder, to the crown of your head.

I sit on the carpet and wait for you to call for the hot towel from the warming case. Throughout the pedicure, the woman sways her head from side to side, eyes half-closed. She moans with relief when you massage her one calf.

When you finish, turning to me for the towel, she leans over, gestures toward her right leg, the nub hovering above the water, dry this whole time.

She says, "Would you mind," and coughs into her arm. "This one also. If it's not too much." She pauses, stares out the window, then down at her lap.

Again, you say nothing—but turn, almost imperceptibly, to her right leg, run a measured caress along the nub's length, before cradling a handful of warm water over the tip, the thin streams crisscrossing the leathered skin. Water droplets. When you're almost done rinsing the soap off, she asks you, gently, almost pleading, to go lower. "If it's the same price anyway," she says. "I can still feel it down there. It's silly, but I can. I can."

You pause—a flicker across your face.

Then, the crow's-feet on your eyes only slightly starker, you wrap your fingers around the air where her calf should be, knead it as if it were fully there. You continue down her invisible foot, rub its bony upper side before cupping the heel with your other hand, pinching along the Achilles' tendon, then stretching the stiff cords along the ankle's underside.

When you turn to me once more, I run to fetch a towel from the case. Without a word, you slide the towel under the phantom limb, pad down the air, the muscle memory in your arms firing the familiar efficient motions, revealing what's not there, the way a conductor's movements make the music somehow more real.

Her foot dry, the woman straps on her prosthesis, rolls down her pant leg, and climbs off. I grab her coat and help her into it. You start walking over to the register when she stops you, places a folded hundred-dollar bill in your palm.

"The lord keep you," she says, eyes lowered—and hobbles out, the bell chime over the door clanging twice as it closes. You stand there, staring at nothing.

Ben Franklin's face darkening in your still wet fingers, you slip the bill under your bra, not the register, then retie your hair.

That night, bellydown on the hardwood, your face resting on a pillow, you asked me to scrape your back. I knelt beside you, peeled your black T-shirt over your shoulders, unhooked your bra. Having done this hundreds of times by now, my hands moved on their own. As the bands fell away, you grabbed the bra, pulled it out from under you, and tossed it aside. Heavy with sweat from the day's work, it landed on the floor with the thud of a knee brace.

The chemicals from the nail salon rose from your skin. I fished a quarter from my pocket, dipped it into the jar of Vicks VapoRub. The bright eucalyptus scent filled the air and you started to relax. I dunked the coin, coating it with the greasy ointment, then dabbed a thumb's worth across your back, down your spine. When your skin shone, I placed the coin at the base of your neck and pulled it outward, across your shoulder blades. I scraped and rescraped in firm, steady strokes, the way you taught me, until russet streaks rose from under the white flesh, the welts deepening into violet grains across your back like new, dark ribs, releasing the bad winds from your body. Through this careful bruising, you heal.

I think of Barthes again. *A writer is someone who plays with the body of his mother,* he says after the death of his own mother, *in order to glorify it, to embellish it.*

How I want this to be true.

And yet, even here, writing you, the physical fact of your body resists my moving it. Even in these sentences, I place my hands on your back and see how dark they are as they lie against the un-changeable white backdrop of your skin. Even now, I see the folds of your waist and hips as I knead out the tensions, the small bones along your spine, a row of ellipses no silence translates. Even after all these years, the contrast between our skin surprises me—the way a blank page does when my hand, gripping a pen, begins to move through its spatial field, trying to act upon its life without marring it. But by writing, I mar it. I change, embellish, and pre-serve you all at once.

You groaned into the pillow as I pressed along your shoulders, then worked down through the stubborn knots. "This is nice. . . . This is so nice." After a while, your breathing deepened, evened out, your arms slack, and you were asleep.

The summer I turned fourteen I got my first job working tobacco on a farm outside Hartford. Most people don't realize tobacco can grow this far north—but put anything near water and it'll green itself to the height of a small army. Still, it's strange how some things come into practice. First cultivated by the Agawam, broadleaf tobacco was soon planted by white settlers as a cash crop after they drove the Natives off the land. And now it's harvested mostly by undocumented immigrants.

I knew you wouldn't let me ride my bike the eight and a half miles out into the country, so I told you I was doing yard work for a church garden on the city outskirts. According to the flyer outside the local YMCA, the job paid nine dollars an hour, which was almost two dollars above minimum wage at the time. And because I was still too young to be legally employed, I was paid under the table, in cash.

It was the summer of 2003, which meant Bush had already declared war on Iraq, citing weapons of mass destruction that never materialized, when the Black Eyed Peas' "Where Is the Love?" played on every radio station but *especially* on PWR 98.6, and you could hear the song from nearly every car on the block if you slept with the windows open, its beats punctuated by the sound of beer bottles bursting on the basketball court across the street, the crackheads lobbing the empties up in the sky, just to see how the streetlights make broken things seem touched by magic, glass sprinkled like glitter on the pavement come morning. It was the summer Tiger Woods would go on to receive the PGA Player of the Year for the fifth time in a row and the Marlins would upset the Yankees (not that I cared or understood), it was two years before Facebook and four before the first iPhone, Steve Jobs was still alive, and your nightmares had just started getting worse, and I'd find you at the kitchen table at some god-awful hour, butt naked, sweating, and counting your tips in order to buy "a secret bunker" just in case, you said, a terrorist attack happened in Hartford. It was the year the *Pioneer 10* spacecraft sent its last signal to NASA before losing contact forever 7.6 billion miles from Earth.

I got up at six in the morning five days a week and rode my bike the full hour it took to get to the farm, crossing the Connecticut River, past the suburbs with their suicidally pristine lawns, then into the sticks. As I approached the property, the fields unfolded all around me on both sides, the telephone wires slacked with the weight of crows dotted along the lines, the sporadic white almond trees in full bloom, irrigation ditches where more than a dozen rabbits would drown by summer's end, their corpses stinking the hot air. Verdant swaths of tobacco, some high as my shoulders, stretched so far that the trees standing at the farm's edge looked more like shrubs. In the middle of it all were three huge unpainted barns, all lined in a row.

I rode up the dirt drive toward the first barn and walked my bike through the opened door. As I adjusted to the cool dark, I saw a row of men sitting along the wall, their dark faces moving over paper plates of runny eggs, talking amongst themselves in Spanish. One of them, seeing me, waved me over, saying something I couldn't catch. When I told him I didn't speak Spanish, he seemed surprised. Then a flare of recognition flicked over him and he lit up. "Ah!" He pointed at me and nodded. "Chinito. ¡Chinito!" I decided, it being my first day, not to correct him. I gave him a thumbs-up. "Sí," I said, smiling, "Chinito."

His name was Manny, he said, and gestured toward a table where a large sheet pan of sunny-side-up eggs sat over a butane heater beside a glass pot of room-temperature coffee. I settled among the men, eating in silence. Not counting myself, there were twenty-two other workers, most of them undocumented migrants from Mexico and Central America save for one, Nico, who was from the Dominican Republic. There was also Rick, a white guy in his twenties from Colchester, who, it was said, was on the sex offender list and tobacco was the only steady job he could get. Most were seasonal workers and followed various crops across the country as they ripened for harvest. At this farm, the men slept in an encampment comprising four trailers set a few yards beyond the tree line at the edge of the property, hidden from the road.

The barn rafters, where the picked tobacco was to be hung to dry, were now empty. By September's end, each barn would house almost two tons of tobacco, two times over. In between bites of runny eggs, I examined the structure. To encourage faster drying, every other wood panel on the barn's siding was raised up, creating rib-like slits, allowing air flow, where the day's heat now ran its hot breath across my neck, carrying with it the sweet-bitter scent of tobacco and the iron of red dirt. The men too smelled of the fields. Before their boots met the soil, their bodies, even after morning showers, exuded the salt and sunbaked underscent from the previous day's work. Soon the same smell would permeate my own pores.

A forest-green Ford Bronco pulled into the drive. The men rose in unison and tossed their plates and cups into the wastebasket. They put on their gloves, some poured water on rags and stuffed them under their caps.

Mr. Buford walked in. A tall, lanky white man of about seventy, he wore a Red Sox cap pulled low over a pair of aviators and a cheddar cheese grin. Hands on his hips, he reminded me of that maniac sergeant in *Full Metal Jacket,* the one who got his brains blown out by one of his own privates for being an asshole. But Buford was cheery enough, charming even, if only a bit forced with it. He grinned, his one gold tooth sparking between his lips, and said, "How's my United Nations this morning? ¿Bueno?"

I walked up to him and introduced myself. I shook his hand, which was rough and chapped, which surprised me. He patted me on the shoulder and said I'll do fine as long as I just follow Manny, my crew leader.

The men and I piled in the back of three pickups and we drove out to the first field, where the crop was tallest, their heavy heads just starting to tilt. We were followed by two tractors, on which the plants would be loaded. By the time we got there, there was already a crew of ten men crouched over the first five rows of tobacco. That was the cut team. Armed with machetes sharpened in the day's first light, they would set out a hundred yards ahead of us and chop down the stalks in quick slashing sweeps. Sometimes, when we worked fast enough, we'd catch up to them, the sound of their blades louder and louder, until you could hear their lungs working as they cut, the stalks falling in bright green splashes around their hunched backs. You could hear the water inside the stems as the steel broke open the membranes, the ground darkening as the plants bled out.

I was on the spear crew, where the shorter workers were. Our task was to pick up the fallen crop, their leaves already shriveled in the sun. We split into teams of three harvesters each, two pickers and one piercer. As a piercer, all you had to do was stand by the spearing horse (a cart with a removable spear attached to it) and run the plants through the spear until the plank filled up. Then you'd remove the spear tip, and one of the pickers would carry the full plank to an idling tractor, where a loader would rack the plank. The piercer would then take another plank from a holster, attach the steel spear tip, and continue filling the new rack.

When the tractor was at capacity, it would be driven back to the barns, where dozens of men, usually the tallest ones, would pass the racks, one by one, to each other up the rafters to dry. Since you could fall from as high as forty feet, the barn was the most dangerous place to work. There were stories the men told, from other farms, how the sound won't leave their ears, the thud of a body—someone humming or talking of the weather or complaining of a woman, the price of gas in Modesto, then the abrupt silence, the leaves shifting where the voice had been.

That first day, I stupidly refused the pair of gloves offered by Manny. They were too big and ran nearly to my elbows. By five o'clock, my hands were so thick and black with sap, dirt, pebbles, and splinters, they resembled the bottom of a pan of burned rice. The crows floated over the field's wrinkled air as we worked the hours bare, their shadows swooping over the land like things falling from the sky. The jackrabbits dipped in and out of the rows, and once in a while a machete would come down on one and you could hear, even through the clink of blades, the shrill yelp of a thing leaving the earth we stood on.

But the work somehow sutured a fracture inside me. A work of unbreakable links and collaboration, each plant cut, picked, lifted, and carried from one container to another in such timely harmony that no stalk of tobacco, once taken from the soil, ever touches ground again. A work of myriad communications, I learned to speak to the men not with my tongue, which was useless there, but with smiles, hand gestures, even silences, hesitations. I made out people, verbs, abstractions, ideas with my fingers, my arms, and by drawing in the dirt.

Manny, brow furrowed, his mustache almost grey from dried sweat, nodded as I cupped my hands into a blossom to indicate your name, Rose.

The most common English word spoken in the nail salon was *sorry.* It was the one refrain for what it meant to work in the service of beauty. Again and again, I watched as manicurists, bowed over a hand or foot of a client, some young as seven, say, "I'm sorry. I'm sorry. I'm so, so sorry," when they had done nothing wrong. I have seen workers, you included, apologize dozens of times throughout a forty-five-minute manicure, hoping to gain warm traction that would lead to the ultimate goal, a tip—only to say *sorry* anyway when none was given.

In the nail salon, *sorry* is a tool one uses to pander until the word itself becomes currency. It no longer merely *apologizes,* but insists, reminds: *I'm here, right here, beneath you.* It is the lowering of oneself so that the client feels right, superior, and charitable. In the nail salon, one's definition of *sorry* is deranged into a new word entirely, one that's charged and reused as both power and defacement at once. Being sorry pays, being sorry even, or especially, when one has no fault, is worth every self-deprecating syllable the mouth allows. Because the mouth must eat.

And yet it's not only so in the nail salon, Ma. In those tobacco fields, too, we said it. "Lo siento," Manny would utter as he walked across Mr. Buford's field of vision. "Lo siento," Rigo whispered as he reached to place a machete back on the wall where Buford sat ticking off numbers on a clipboard. "Lo siento," I said to the boss after missing a day when Lan had another schizophrenic attack and had shoved all her clothes into the oven, saying she had to get rid of the "evidence." "Lo siento," we said when, one day, night arrived only to find the field half harvested, the tractor, its blown-out engine, sitting in the stilled dark. "Lo siento, señor," each of us said as we walked past the truck with Buford inside blasting Hank Williams and staring at his withered crop, a palm-sized photo of Ronald Reagan taped to the dash. How the day after, we began work not with "Good morning" but with "Lo siento." The phrase with its sound of a bootstep sinking, then lifted, from mud. The slick muck of it wetting our tongues as we apologized ourselves back to making our living. Again and again, I write to you regretting my tongue.

I think of those men who sweated, who joked and sang beside me in the endless tobacco. How George was one grand away, about two months of work, from buying his mother a house outside Guadalajara. How Brandon was going to send his sixteen-year-old daughter, Lucinda, to university in Mexico City to be a dentist, like she always wanted. How after one more season, Manny would be back by the seaside village in El Salvador, running his fingers over the scar on his mother's collarbone where a tumor would've just been removed using the pay he received removing tobacco from the Connecticut soil. How he'd buy, with his remaining savings, a boat and try his luck fishing for marlins. *Sorry,* for these men, was a passport to remain.

The day's work done, my white tank top so stained with dirt and sweat, it was like I wore no shirt at all as I walked my bike out of the barn. Fingers sticky and raw over the handlebars, I plunged my silver Huffy forward, down the dust-blown street, past the vast and now empty distances where the crop once stood, the sun burning low above the tree line. And I heard them behind me, their voices distinct as channels on a radio. "¡Hasta mañana, Chinito!" "¡Adios, muchacho!" And I knew which men the voices belonged to. Without looking, I could tell Manny was waving, like he did each day, his three-and-a-half-fingered hand black against the last light.

What I wanted to say to them, as I rode away, and also the next morning, all mornings, is what I want to say to you now: *Sorry.* Sorry that it would be so long before they would see their loved ones, that some might not make it back across the desert border alive, taken by dehydration and exposure or murdered by drug cartels or the right-wing crack militia in Texas and Arizona. *Lo siento,* I wanted to say. But I couldn't. Because by then my *sorry* had already changed into something else. It had become a portion of my own name—unutterable without fraudulence.

Which is why, when the boy came to me one afternoon, the boy who would change what I knew of summer, how deep a season opens when you refuse to follow the days out of it, I said "Sorry."

The boy from whom I learned there was something even more brutal and total than work—want. That August, in the fields, it was he who came into my vision. Near day's end, I felt another worker beside me but, caught in the rhythm of the harvest, couldn't stop to consider him. We picked for about ten minutes, his presence intensifying on the periphery until he stepped in front of me as I reached to lift a wilted stalk. I looked up at him, a head taller, his finely boned face dirt-streaked under a metal army helmet, tipped slightly backward, as if he had just walked out from one of Lan's stories and into my hour, somehow smiling.

"Trevor," he said, straightening up. "I'm Trevor." I would know only later that he was Buford's grandson, working the farm to get away from his vodka-soaked old man. And because I am your son, I said, "Sorry." Because I am your son, my apology had become, by then, an extension of myself. It was my *Hello*.

That first day after meeting him in the field, I found Trevor again in the barn. The dusked light had washed the interior with a bluish glow. Outside, the workers' axes clinked against their belt straps as they climbed the dirt knoll back to their Airstreams by the edge of the wood. The air was cool, tinged with chlorophyll from the fresh-cut tobacco now suspended from the beams above us, some still dripping, making tiny dust swirls along the barn floor.

I don't know why I lingered at my bike, taking time checking the spokes. Trevor sat on a bench along the wall, chugging a neon-yellow Gatorade.

There was something about the way he looked when lost in thought, his brow pinched under squinted eyes, giving his boyish face the harsh, hurt expression of someone watching his favorite dog being put down too soon. The way his mud-streaked and dusty edges juxtaposed against that rounded mouth and pert lips sealed into a flushed, feminine pout. Who are you, I thought to myself as I worked the brakes.

What I felt then, however, was not desire, but the coiled charge of its possibility, a feeling that emitted, it seemed, its own gravity, holding me in place. The way he watched me back there in the field, when we worked briefly, side by side, our arms brushing against each other as the plants racked themselves in a green blur before me, his eyes lingering, then flitting away when I caught them. I was seen—I who had seldom been seen by anyone. I who was taught, by you, to be invisible in order to be safe, who, in elementary school, was sent to the fifteen-minute time-out in the corner only to be found two hours later, when everyone was long gone and Mrs. Harding, eating lunch at her desk, peered over her macaroni salad and gasped. "My god! My god, I forgot you were still here! What are you still doing here?"

Trevor and I talked about the fields as the light slipped from the barn, how much more there was to be done, how the crop was for cigars exported to Africa and East Asia, where smoking was still popular and where anything that came from America still had an aura of promise to it. But truth was, Trevor said, the crop was low-grade, the burn bitter in the throat, sour.

"This crop ain't even legit," he said. His voice echoed up the rafters. I peered over my shoulder, catching him. "Wormholes all over 'em. We got two good years, maybe three, and then—" He ran his hand, like a blade, over his Adam's apple. "It's a wrap." He grew silent. I could feel his eyes as I returned to my bike. And I wanted it, for his gaze to fix me to the world I felt only halfway inside of.

As I laid my chain on the fulcrum, I could hear the swooshing of the Gatorade in the bottle, then the bottle being set down on the bench. After a moment, he said, real quiet, "I fucking hate my dad."

Up until then I didn't think a white boy could hate anything about his life. I wanted to know him through and through, by that very hate. Because that's what you give anyone who sees you, I thought. You take their hatred head-on, and you cross it, like a bridge, to face them, to enter them.

"I hate my dad, too," I said to my hands, now still and dark with chain grease.

When I turned around Trevor was smiling up at the ceiling. He saw me, hopped off the ledge, and walked over, the smile fading into something else as he pulled the army helmet over his eyes. The black Adidas logo on his white T-shirt shifted as he approached. I was a freshman that summer, and Trevor was already a junior. Although barely visible in the sun, here in the barn, and coming closer, his thin mustache deepened, a blondish streak dark with sweat. And above that, his eyes: their grey irises smattered with bits of brown and ember so that, looking at them, you could almost see, right behind you, something burning under an overcast sky. It seemed the boy was always looking at a plane wrecking itself midair. That's what I saw that first day. And although I knew that nothing behind me was on fire, I turned back anyway and saw the coiled summer air, sputtering with heat, rise over the razed fields.

The boy is six and wearing nothing but a pair of white underwear with Supermans patterned everywhere. You know this story. He has just finished crying and is now entering that state where his jaw shudders to calm itself shut. His snot-plastered nose, its salt on his lips, his tongue, he's at home. His mother, you remember this, has locked him in the basement for wetting his bed again, the four or five Supermans near his crotch now soiled dark. She had dragged him out of bed by the arm, then down the stairs as he screamed, begged, "One more chance, Ma. One more chance." The kind of basement no one goes down, all around him the dank scent of damp earth, rusted pipes choked with cobwebs, his own piss still wet down his leg, between his toes. He stands with one foot on the other, as if touching less of the basement meant he was less inside it. He closes his eyes. This is my superpower, he thinks: to make a dark even darker than what's around me. He stops crying.

Summer was almost gone as we sat on the toolshed roof by the field's edge, but the heat had stayed, and our shirts clung to us like unmolted skins. The tin roof, touched all day by the heat, was still warm through my shorts. The sun, now waning, must still be stronger somewhere west, I thought, like in Ohio, golden yet for some boy I'll never meet.

I thought of that boy, how far from me he was and still American. The wind was cool and thick up the legs of my shorts.

We were talking, as we did those days after work when we were too exhausted to head home just yet. We talked about his guns, of school, how he might drop out, how the Colt factory in Windsor might be hiring again now that the latest shooting spree was three months done and already old news, we talked of the next game out on Xbox, his old man, his old man's drinking, we talked of sunflowers, how goofy they looked, like cartoons, Trevor said, but real. We talked about you, about your nightmares, your loosening mind, his face troubled as he listened, which made his pout more defined.

A long silence. Then Trevor took out his cell phone, snapped a picture at the colors at the sky's end, then put it back in his pocket without reviewing what he took. Our eyes met. He flashed an embarrassed smile, then looked away and started picking at a pimple on his chin.

"Cleopatra," he said after a while.

"What?"

"Cleopatra saw the same sunset. Ain't that crazy? Like everybody who was ever alive only seen one sun." He gestured to indicate the whole town, even though we were the only people there far as the eye could see. "No wonder people used to think it was god himself."

"Said who?"

"People." He chewed his lip for a moment. "Sometimes I wanna just go that way forever." He pointed his chin beyond the sycamores. "Like just *psssh*." I studied his arm propped behind him, the thin, flowing muscles, field-toned and burger-fed, shifting as he talked.

I flung the last rind from the grapefruit I was peeling off the roof. What about our skeletons, I wanted to ask, how do we get away from them—but thought better of it. "It must suck to be the sun, though," I said, handing him a pink half.

He put the whole half in his mouth. "Hob bob?"

"Finish chewing you animal."

He rolled back his eyes and bobbled his head playfully, as if possessed, the clear juice dripping down his chin, his neck, the indent under his Adam's apple, no larger than a thumbprint, glistening. He swallowed, wiped his mouth with the back of his arm. "How come?" he repeated, serious.

"'Cause you never see yourself if you're the sun. You don't even know where you are in the sky." I placed a wedge on my tongue, letting the acid sting the place where I'd bit the inside of my cheek all week for no reason.

He looked at me thoughtfully, turned the idea in his head, his lips wet with juice.

"Like you don't even know if you're round or square or even if you're ugly or not," I continued. I wanted it to sound important, urgent—but had no idea if I believed it. "Like you can only see what you *do* to the earth, the colors and stuff, but not who you are." I glanced at him.

He picked at a hole in his grass-stained white Vans. His nail scraped at the leather in the sneaker, the hole widening.

I hadn't noticed, until then, the crickets chirping. The day dimmed around us.

Trevor said, "I think it sucks to be the sun 'cause he's on fire." I heard what I thought was another cricket, a closer one. The throb, a thudded beating. But Trevor, still sitting, legs spread, had let his penis, soft and pink, hang out from the pant leg of his shorts, and was now pissing. The stream rattled on the slanted metal roof before falling off the side, dribbling onto the dirt below. "And I'm putting out the fire," he said, his lips curled in concentration.

I turned away, but kept seeing him, not Trevor, but the boy in Ohio, the one who will soon be found by the hour I had just passed through, unscathed. Together, with nothing to say, we spat, one by one, the grapefruit seeds stored in our cheeks. They fell on the tin roof in big fat drops and blued as the sun sank fully behind the trees.

One day, after overtime at the clock factory, the boy's mother came home to a house littered with hundreds of toy soldiers, their curled plastic lives spread like debris across the kitchen tiles. The boy usually knew to clean up before she came home. But this day he was lost in the story he made of their bodies. The men were in the midst of saving a six-inch Mickey Mouse trapped in a prison made of black VHS tapes.

When the door opened, the boy leapt to his feet but it was too late. Before he could make out his mother's face, the backhand blasted the side of his head, followed by another, then more. A rain of it. A storm of mother. The boy's grandmother, hearing the screams, rushed in and, as if by instinct, knelt on all fours over the boy, making a small and feeble house with her frame. Inside it, the boy curled into his clothes and waited for his mother to calm. Through his grandmother's trembling arms, he noticed the videocassettes had toppled over. Mickey Mouse was free.

A few days after the shed roof, the grapefruit, I found myself sitting shotgun in Trevor's truck. He fished the Black & Mild from the chest pocket of his T-shirt, laid it gently across his kneecaps. Then he grabbed the box cutter from his other pocket and cut a lengthwise slit along the cigarillo before emptying its contents out the window. "Open the glove," he said. "Yeah. No, under the insurance. Yeah, right there."

I grabbed the two dime bags, one half-filled with weed, the other with coke, and handed them to him. He opened the bag, placed the weed, already broken, into the gutted cigarillo till it filled. He threw the bag out the window, then opened the second bag, tipped the white grains over the row of weed. "Like snow-capped mountains!" he said, grinning. In his excitement, he let the second bag fall through his legs, to the floorboard. He licked the Black & Mild's hem, sealing the slit until it stuck into a tight joint, then blew on the hem, waved the joint in front of him to dry. He marveled at it between his fingers before placing it between his lips and lighting. We sat there, passing it back and forth until my head felt thin and skull-less.

After what seemed like hours, we ended up in the barn, somehow lying on the dusty floor. It must have been late—or at least dark enough to make the barn's interior feel immense, like the hull of a beached ship.

"Don't be weird," Trevor said, sitting up. He grabbed the WWII army helmet off the floor and put it back on, the one he was wearing the day I met him. I keep seeing that helmet—but this can't be right. This boy, impossibly American and alive in the image of a dead soldier. It's too neat, so clean a symbol I must have made it up. And even now, in all the pictures I looked through, I can't find him wearing it. Yet here it is, tilted to hide Trevor's eyes, making him seem anonymous and easy to look at. I studied him like a new word. His reddish lips stuck out from the helmet's visor. The Adam's apple, oddly small, a blip in a line drawn by a tired artist. It was dark enough for my eyes to swallow all of him without ever seeing him clearly. Like eating with the lights off—it still nourished even if you didn't know where your body ends.

"Don't be weird."

"I wasn't looking at you," I said, diverting my gaze. "I was just thinking."

"Look. The radio's working again." He played with the knob on the handheld radio in his lap and the static intensified, then a robust and urgent voice poured into the space between us: *Fourth down-and-goal with twenty-seven seconds to go and the Patriots line up for the snap . . .*

"Nice! We're back in this." He struck his palm with his fist, teeth clenched: a greyish flash under the helmet.

He was looking up, visualizing the game, the field, his blue-and-grey Patriots. My eyes dilated, I took him in deeper, the pale sweep of his jaw, his throat, the thin adolescent cords rising along its length. His shirt was off because it was summer. Because it didn't matter. There were two fingers of dirt on his collarbone from earlier that afternoon, when we planted the baby apple tree in Buford's backyard.

"Are we close?" I asked, not knowing what I meant.

The voices roared, straining through the crackle.

"Yeah. I think we got this." He lay back, beside me, the dirt crunching under his weight. "Okay, so fourth down basically means this is our last chance—are you with me?"

"Uh-huh."

"Then why you staring at the ceiling?"

"I'm with you." I propped my head up with my palm and faced him—his torso a faint blaze in the half-dark. "I'm with you, Trev. Fourth down."

"Don't call me that. It's Trevor. Full and long, alright?"

"Sorry."

"It's fine. *Fourth down* means it's all or bust."

On our backs, shoulders almost touching, the thin film of heat formed between our skins as the air thickened with the men's voices, the crowd's corrosive cheers.

"We got this. We got this," his voice said. His lips moved, I imagined, the way they do in prayer. It seemed he could see through the roof, to the starless sky—the moon that night a gnawed bone above the field. I don't know if it was him or me who shifted. But the space between us grew thinner and thinner as the game roared on, and our upper arms grew moist, touched so lightly neither of us noticed it happening. And maybe it was there in the barn that I first saw what I would always see when flesh is pressed against the dark. How the sharper edges of his body—shoulders, elbows, chin, and nose—poked through the blackness, a body halfway in, or out of, a river's surface.

The Patriots soared through their winning touchdown. The crickets ignited across the low shifting grass around the barn. Turning to him, I felt their serrated legs through the floor beneath us as I said his name, full and long; I said it so quiet the syllables never survived my mouth. I drew closer, toward the wet salted heat of his cheek. He made a sound almost like pleasure—or maybe I just imagined that. I went on, licking his chest, his ribs, the flare of hair on his pale belly. And then the heavy *clank* as the helmet tipped backward, the crowd roaring.

In the bathroom with the pea-soup walls, the grandma rolls a freshly boiled egg over the boy's face where, a few minutes ago, his mother had flung an empty ceramic teapot that exploded on the boy's cheek.

The egg is warm as my insides, he thinks. It's an old remedy. "The egg, it heals even the worst bruises," says his grandma. She works on the violet lump shining, like a plum, on the boy's face. As the egg circled, its smooth pressure on the bruise, the boy watched, under a puffed lid, his grandma's lips crease with focus as she worked. Years later, as a young man, when all that remains of the grandma is a face etched in his mind, the boy will remember that crease between her lips while breaking open a hard-boiled egg on his desk on a winter night in New York. Short on rent, it would be eggs for dinner for the rest of the week. They would not be warm, but cold in his palm, having been boiled by the dozen earlier that morning.

At his desk, drifting, he'll roll the moist egg across his cheek. Without speaking, he will say *Thank you.* He'll keep saying it until the egg grows warm with himself.

"Thank you, Grandma," says the boy, squinting.

"You fine now, Little Dog." She lifts the pearly orb, and places it gently to his lips. "Eat," she says. "Swallow. Your bruises are inside it now. Swallow and it won't hurt anymore." And so he eats. He is eating still.

There were colors, Ma. Yes, there were colors I felt when I was with him. Not words—but shades, penumbras.

We stopped the truck one time on the side of a dirt road and sat against the driver door, facing a meadow. Soon our shadows on the red exterior shifted and bloomed, like purple graffiti. Two double-cheese Whoppers were warming on the hood, their parchment wrappers crackling. Did you ever feel colored-in when a boy found you with his mouth? What if the body, at its best, is only a *longing* for body? The blood racing to the heart only to be sent back out, filling the routes, the once empty channels, the miles it takes to take us toward each other. Why did I feel more myself while reaching for him, my hand midair, than I did having touched him?

His tongue tracing my ear: the green pulled through a blade of grass.

The burgers started to smoke. We let them.

I would work for the farm for two more summers after that first one—but my time with Trevor would stretch through all the seasons in between. And that day, it was October 16—a Thursday. Partly cloudy, the leaves crisp but still on their branches.

We had eggs sautéed in diced tomatoes and fish sauce over rice for dinner. I was wearing a grey-red plaid button-up from L.L.Bean. You were in the kitchen, washing up, humming. The TV was on, playing a rerun of *Rugrats,* Lan clapping to the animated show. One of the bulbs in the bathroom buzzed, the wattage too strong for the socket. You wanted to go buy new ones at the drugstore but decided to wait for your wages from the salon so we could also get a box of Ensure for Lan. You were okay that day. You even smiled twice through the cigarette smoke. I remember it. I remember it all because how can you forget anything about the day you first found yourself beautiful?

I turned the shower off and, instead of toweling and dressing before the steam on the door mirror cleared, like I normally would, I waited. It was an accident, my beauty revealed to me. I was daydreaming, thinking about the day before, of Trevor and me behind the Chevy, and had stood in the tub with the water off for too long. By the time I stepped out, the boy before the mirror stunned me.

Who was he? I touched the face, its sallow cheeks. I felt my neck, the braid of muscles sloped to collarbones that jutted into stark ridges. The scraped-out ribs sunken as the skin tried to fill its irregular gaps, the sad little heart rippling underneath like a trapped fish. The eyes that wouldn't match, one too open, the other dazed, slightly lidded, cautious of whatever light was given it. It was everything I hid from, everything that made me want to be a sun, the only thing I knew that had no shadow. And yet, I stayed. I let the mirror hold those flaws—because for once, drying, they were not wrong to me but something that was wanted, that was sought and found among a landscape as enormous as the one I had been lost in all this time. Because the thing about beauty is that it's only beautiful outside of itself. Seen through a mirror, I viewed my body as another, a boy a few feet away, his expression unmoved, daring the skin to remain as it was, as if the sun, setting, was not already elsewhere, was not in Ohio.

I got what I wanted—a boy swimming toward me. Except I was no shore, Ma. I was driftwood trying to remember what I had broken from to get here.

Back in the barn that first night we touched, the Patriots game at halftime through the radio, I heard him. The air was thick or thin or not there. Maybe we even drifted off for a bit. The commercials were on, crackling and buzzing through the receiver, but I heard him. We were just staring at the rafters, and then he said, casually, as if naming a country on a map, "Why was I born?" His features troubled in the waning light.

I pretended not to hear.

But he said it again. "Why was I even born, Little Dog?" The radio hissed beneath his voice. And I spoke to the air. I said, "I hate KFC," responding to the commercial, on purpose.

"Me too," he said without skipping a beat.

And we cracked up. We cracked open. We fell apart like that, laughing.

Trevor and his daddy lived alone in an Easter-yellow mobile home behind the interstate. That afternoon his old man was out laying redbrick walkways for a commercial park out in Chesterfield. The white door frames in the mobile home were stained pink with fingerprints: a house colored with work, which meant a house colored with exhaustion, disrepair. The rug uprooted "so no one gotta clean," but the hardwood never waxed and polished, and you could feel the hammered-down nails through your socks. The cabinet doors were torn off "to make it easy." There was a cinder block under the sink to hold the pipes. In the living room, above the couch, was a duct-taped poster of Neil Young, guitar in hand, grimacing into a song I've never heard.

In his room, Trevor turned on a Sony car stereo hooked to two speakers set on a dresser, and bobbed his head as a hip-hop beat intensified through the amp. The beats were interspersed with recordings of gunshots, men shouting, a car peeling off.

"Have you heard this yet? It's this new dude 50 Cent." Trevor smiled. "Pretty dope, huh?" A bird flew past the window, making the room seem to blink.

"I've never heard of him," I lied—why I'm not quite sure. Maybe I wanted to give him the power of this small knowledge over me. But I'd heard it before, many times, as it was played that year through endless passing cars and opened apartment windows back in Hartford. The entire album, *Get Rich or Die Tryin'*, was burned bootleg on hundreds of blank CDs bought in forty packs for cheap from Walmart or Target—so that the whole northside echoed with a kind of anthem of Curtis Jackson's voice fading in and out of intelligibility as you rode your bike through the streets.

"*I walk the block with the bundles,*" he recited, his hands gestured in front of him, fingers splayed. "*I've been knocked on the humble, swing the ox when I rumble, show your ass what my gun do."*

He paced the room, rapping with purpose, gusto, frowning as spit sprayed the air, landed cool on my cheek. "Come on, man. I love this part." He mouthed the words, staring at me as if I were the camera in the music video. I followed his lips until we were singing the hook together, my shoulders swaying to the rhythm. *"Many men, many, many, many, many men. Wish death 'pon me. Lord I don't cry no more, don't look to the sky no more. Have mercy on me."*

In that room, among the *Star Wars* poster (*The Empire Strikes Back*) peeling above his unmade bed, among the empty root beer cans, the twenty-pound dumbbell, one half of a broken skateboard, the desk covered with loose change, empty gum packets, gas station receipts, weed crumbs, fentanyl patches and empty dime bags, coffee mugs ringed brown with old water and joint roaches, a copy of *Of Mice and Men,* empty shell casings from a Smith & Wesson, there were no questions. Under the covers, we made friction of each other and fiction of everything else. He had shaved his head in the sink that day and the bits of hair pricked us everywhere we moved, our fingers lost around belt buckles. A Band-Aid, loosened from sweat and heat, hung from his elbow, its plastic film scraping my ribs as he climbed on top of me, searching. Under my fingers, the stretch marks above his knees, on his shoulders, and the base of his spine shone silver and new. He was a boy breaking out and into himself at once. That's what I wanted—not merely the body, desirable as it was, but its will to grow into the very world that rejects its hunger. Then I wanted more, the scent, the atmosphere of him, the taste of French fries and peanut butter underneath the salve of his tongue, the salt around his neck from the two-hour drives to nowhere and a Burger King at the edge of the county, a day of tense talk with his old man, the rust from the electric razor he shared with that old man, how I would always find it on his sink in its sad plastic case, the tobacco, weed and cocaine on his fingers mixed with motor oil, all of it accumulating into the afterscent of wood smoke caught and soaked in his hair, as if when he came to me, his mouth wet and wanting, he came from a place on fire, a place he could never return to.

And what do you do to a boy like that but turn yourself into a doorway, a place he can go through again and again, each time entering the same room? Yes, I wanted it all. I drove my face into him as if into a climate, the autobiography of a season. Until I was numb. "Close your eyes," he said, shaking. "Don't want you seeing me like this." But I opened them anyway, knowing that in the dim, everything looked the same. Like you're still sleeping. But in our hurry, our teeth collided. He made a hurt sound, then turned away, suddenly embarrassed. Before I could ask if he was okay, he resumed, his eyes half-open as we locked, slick and smooth now, deeper. Then lower, toward the waistband's elastic resistance, the snap never coming, the fabric's rustle at my ankles, my cock, the bead of moisture at its tip the coldest thing between us.

Surfacing from the sheets, his face shone through the wet mask we made of our scavenge. He was white, I never forgot this. He was always white. And I knew this was why there was a space for us: a farm, a field, a barn, a house, an hour, two. A space I never found in the city, where the tenement apartments we lived in were so cramped one could tell when a neighbor had a stomach flu in the middle of the night. To hide here, in a room in a broken-down mobile home, was, somehow, a privilege, a chance. He was white. I was yellow. In the dark, our facts lit us up and our acts pinned us down.

But how do I tell you about that boy without telling you about the drugs that soon blew it apart, the Oxy and coke, the way they made the world smolder at its tips? And then the rust-red Chevy? The one Buford gave his son, Trev's old man, when he was twenty-four, the one the old man cherished, having repaired and replaced enough parts to make four trucks over through the years. How its windows were already blue-streaked and its tires smooth as human skin by the time we blasted through the corn, going fifty-five as Trevor shouted crazy, a patch of fentanyl hot on his arm, the liquid melted through its edges and dripping down his bicep like sick sap. Cocaine in our noses, our lungs, we laughed, in a way. And then the swerve, a smithereen of yellow, the slam, glass skittering, the crushed hood smoking under the dead oak. A red line running down Trevor's cheek, then widening at his jaw. Then his daddy calling from the house, the rage in his scream jolting us from the seats.

As the engine steamed, we felt our ribs for broken bones, then bolted out of the gasoline-reeked pickup, crossed the rest of the cornfield behind Trevor's house, past the wheelless John Deere tractor suspended on cinder blocks, the empty chicken coop with latches rusted shut, over the small plastic white fence invisible under a choke of brambles, then through crabgrass and under the highway overpass, toward the pines. Dry leaves crashing past us. Trevor's old man running toward the wrecked truck, the only car they owned, neither of us with the guts to look back.

How do I tell you about Trevor without telling you, again, of those pines? How it was an hour after the Chevy that we lay there, the cold seeping up from the forest floor. How we sang "This Little Light of Mine" until the blood on our faces grabbed around our lips and stiffened us quiet.

The first time we fucked, we didn't fuck at all. I only have the nerve to tell you what comes after because the chance this letter finds you is slim—the very impossibility of your reading this is all that makes my telling it possible.

In Trevor's mobile home, there was a painting of a bowl of peaches in the hallway that always caught me. The hallway was too narrow and you could only see it from inches away, more aftermath than art. I had to stand a little to the side to see it in full. Each time I walked by I slowed down, taking it in. A cheap painting from Family Dollar, mass-produced with vague indications of impressionism. When I examined the brushstrokes, I saw that they were not painted on at all, but printed on with speckled relief, suggesting a hand without enacting the real. The relief "strokes" never cohered with their shades, so that a stroke would hold two, even three colors at once. A fake. A fraud. Which was why I loved it. The materials never suggested authenticity, but rather, an inconspicuous sameness, a desire to pass as art only under the most cursory glance. It hung on the wall, hidden in the gloomy hallway that led to Trevor's room. I never asked who put it there. Peaches. Pink peaches.

Under the humid sheets, he pressed his cock between my legs. I spat in my hand and reached back, grabbed tight his heated length, mimicking the real thing, as he pushed. I glanced back and caught the thrilled mischief in his eyes. Although this was a mock attempt, a penis in a fist in place of the inner self, for a moment it *was* real. It was real because we didn't have to look—as if we fucked and unfucked at a distance from our bodies, yet still inside the sensation, like a memory.

We did what we had seen in porn. I wrapped my free arm around his neck, my mouth searching and taking any part of Trevor that was closest, and he did the same, pressing his nose into the crook of my neck. His tongue, his tongues. And his arms, hot along their tense muscles, reminded me of the neighbor's house on Franklin Ave. the morning after it burned. I had lifted a piece of window frame, still warm, from the wreck, my fingers digging into the soft wood, damp from the hydrant, the way I now dug into Trevor's bicep. I thought I heard the hiss of steam coming off him, but it was only October slashing outside, wind making a lexicon of the leaves.

We did not speak.

He fucked my hand until he shuddered, wet, like the muffler of a truck starting up in the rain. Until my palm slickened and he said, "No, oh no," as if it was blood, not semen, that was leaving him. Done with ourselves, we lay for a while, our faces cooling as they dried.

Now, whenever I visit a museum, I'm hesitant to come too close to a painting for fear of what I might, or might not, find there. Like the pinkish smear of Trevor's dollar-store peaches, I stare instead, hands behind my back, from far away, sometimes even at the room's threshold, where everything is still possible because nothing is revealed.

Afterward, lying next to me with his face turned away, he cried skillfully in the dark. The way boys do. The first time we fucked, we didn't fuck at all.

The boy is standing in a tiny yellow kitchen in Hartford. Still a toddler, the boy laughs, believing they are dancing. He remembers this—because who can forget the first memory of their parents? It was not until the blood ran from his mother's nose, turning her white shirt the color of Elmo he had seen on *Sesame Street,* that he started to scream. Then his grandmother rushed in, grabbed him, and ran past her reddening daughter, the man shouting over her, out to the balcony, then down the back steps, shouting in Vietnamese, "He's killing my girl! God, god! He's killing her." People ran from all over, from their stoops down the block to the three-story apartment; Tony the mechanic from across the street with the wrecked arm, Junior's father, Miguel, and Roger, who lived above the convenience store. They all rushed over and pulled the father off his mother.

The ambulances came, the boy, hoisted to his grandmother's hip, watched the officers approach his father with guns drawn, how his father waved a bloody twenty-dollar bill, the way he did back in Saigon where the cops would take the money, tell the boy's mother to calm down and take a walk, then leave as if nothing happened. The boy watched as the American officers tackled his father, the money slipping out in the tussle and landing on the sidewalk lit by sulfur lights. Focused on the brown-and-green money-leaf on the pavement, half expecting it to fly up, back onto a winter tree, the boy did not see his father cuffed, dragged up to his feet, his head pushed into the patrol car. He saw only the crumpled money, until a neighbor girl in pigtails swiped it when no one was looking. The boy looked up to find his mother being carried out by paramedics, her broken face floating past him on the stretcher.

In his backyard, an empty dirt field beside a freeway overpass, I watched Trevor aim his .32 Winchester at a row of paint cans lined on an old park bench. I did not know then what I know now: to be an American boy, and then an American boy with a gun, is to move from one end of a cage to another.

He tugged at the visor of his Red Sox cap, his lips scrunched. A porch light reflected on the barrel a small white star in the faraway-dark, which rose and fell as he aimed. This is what we did on nights like this, a Saturday with no sound for miles. I sat on a milk crate sipping Dr Pepper and watched him empty one cartridge after another into metal. Where the rifle's butt recoiled against his shoulder, his green Whalers T-shirt wrinkled, the creases grabbing with each shot.

The cans leaped one by one off the bench. I watched, recalling a story Mr. Buford told us back on the farm. Years ago, hunting in Montana, Buford found a moose in his trap. A male. He spoke slowly, rubbing his white stubble, describing how the trap had cut off the moose's hind leg—a sound like a wet stick snapping, he said—save for a few stringy pink ligaments. The animal groaned against its body, which, bleeding and torn, was suddenly a prison. It raged, fat tongue lolling out a voice. "Almost like a man's," Buford said, "like you and me." He glanced at his grandson, then at the ground, his plate of beans speckled with ants.

He put down his rifle, he explained, and took out the double barrel holstered to his back and steadied. But the buck noticed him and charged, tearing its leg clean off. It ran right at him before he could aim, then veered toward a clearing and broke through the trees, hobbling on what was left of itself.

Like you and me, I said to no one.

"I got lucky," Buford said. "Three legs be damned, those things can kill ya."

In the backyard, Trevor and I sat on the grass, passing a joint sprinkled with crushed Oxy. With the back blown clean off, only the legs remained of the bench. Four legs, without a body.

A week after the first time, we did it again. His cock in my hand, we began. My grip tightened around the covers. And that inertia of his skin, damp-tight against my own, made the task feel, not merely of fucking, but of hanging on. The inside of his cheek, where the flesh was softest, tasted like cinnamon gum and wet stones. I reached down and felt the cockslit. When I rubbed the warming globe, he shivered against himself. Out of nowhere, he grabbed my hair, my head jerked back in his grip. I let out a clipped yelp, and he stopped, his hand hovering beside my face, hesitant.

"Keep going," I said, and leaned back, offering it all. "Grab it."

I can't make sense of what I felt. The force and torque, of pain gathered toward a breaking point, a sensation I never imagined was a part of sex. Something took over and I told him to do it harder. And he did. He lifted me nearly off the bed by the roots of my follicles. With each slam, a light turned on and off inside me. I flickered, like a bulb in a storm, seeking myself in his steering. He let go of my hair only to put his arm under my neck. My lips brushed his forearm and I could taste the salt concentrated there. Recognition flinched inside him. This is how we were going to do it from now on.

What do you call the animal that, finding the hunter, offers itself to be eaten? A martyr? A weakling? No, a beast gaining the rare agency to stop. Yes, the period in the sentence—it's what makes us human, Ma, I swear. It lets us stop in order to keep going.

Because submission, I soon learned, was also a kind of power. To be inside of pleasure, Trevor needed me. I had a choice, a craft, whether he ascends or falls depends on my willingness to make room for him, for you cannot rise without having something to rise over. Submission does not require elevation in order to control. I lower myself. I put him in my mouth, to the base, and peer up at him, my eyes a place he might flourish. After a while, it is the cocksucker who moves. And he follows, when I sway this way he swerves along. And I look up at him as if looking at a kite, his entire body tied to the teetering world of my head.

He loves me, he loves me not, we are taught to say, as we tear the flower away from its flowerness. To arrive at love, then, is to arrive through obliteration. Eviscerate me, we mean to say, and I'll tell you the truth. I'll say yes. "Keep going," I begged. "Fuck me up, fuck me up." By then, violence was already mundane to me, was what I knew, ultimately, of love. Fuck. Me. Up. It felt good to name what was already happening to me all my life. I was being fucked up, at last, by choice. In Trevor's grip, I had a say in how I would be taken apart. So I said it: "Harder. Harder," until I heard him gasp, as if surfacing from a nightmare we swore was real.

After he came, when he tried to hold me, his lips on my shoulder, I pushed him away, pulled my boxers on, and went to rinse my mouth.

Sometimes being offered tenderness feels like the very proof that you've been ruined.

Then, one afternoon, out of nowhere, Trevor asked me to top him, the way we had been doing it, which we now called *fake fucking*. He lay on his side. I spat in my palm and snuggled up to him. I was only up to his neck in height, but lying down, spooning, our heads met. I kissed his shoulders, made my way to his neck, where his hair ended, as some boys' do, with the strands whittled down to a small half-inch tail at the nape. It was the part that shone like wheat-tips touched by sunlight, while the rest of his head, with its fuller hair, stayed dark brown. I flicked my tongue under it. How could such a hard-stitched boy possess something so delicate, made entirely of edges, of endings? Between my lips, it was a bud sprouted from inside him, possible. This part is the good part of Trevor, I thought. Not the squirrel shooter. Not the one who axed up what was left of the shot-up park bench to splinters. The one who, in a fit of rage I can't recall the cause of, shoved me into a snowbank on our walk back from the corner store. This part, this flick of hair, was what made him stop his truck in the middle of traffic to stare at a six-foot sunflower on the side of the road, his mouth slack. Who told me sunflowers were his favorite because they grew higher than people. Who ran his fingers so gently down their lengths I thought red blood pulsed inside the stalks.

But it was over before it began. Before my tip brushed his greased palm, he tensed, his back a wall. He pushed me back, sat up. "Fuck." He stared straight ahead.

"I can't. I just—I mean . . ." He spoke into the wall. "I dunno. I don't wanna feel like a girl. Like a bitch. I can't, man. I'm sorry, it's not for me—" He paused, wiped his nose. "It's for you. Right?"

I pulled the covers to my chin.

I had thought sex was to breach new ground, despite terror, that as long as the world did not see us, its rules did not apply. But I was wrong.

The rules, they were already inside us.

Soon the Super Nintendo was on. Trevor's shoulders shook as he hammered away at the controller. "Hey. Hey, Little Dog," he said after a while. Then, softly, still fixed on the game: "I'm sorry. Okay?"

On the screen, a tiny red Mario jumped from platform to platform. If Mario fell off, he would have to start the level over, from the beginning. This was also called dying.

The boy ran away from home one night. He ran with no plans. In his backpack were a bag of Cheerios taken out the box, a pair of socks, and two *Goosebumps* paperbacks. Although he could not read chapter books yet, he knew how far a story could take him, and holding these books meant there were at least two more worlds he could eventually step into. But because he was ten, he made it only to the playscape behind his elementary school twenty minutes away.

After sitting on the swings for a while in the dark, the creaking chain the only sound, he climbed one of the nearby maples. The leafy branches jostled around him as he climbed. Halfway up, he stopped and listened to the neighborhood, a pop song coming from an apartment window across the lot, traffic from the nearby freeway, a woman calling in a dog or a child.

Then the boy heard footsteps on dried leaves. He pulled his knees up close and hugged the trunk. He held still and stared down, cautious, through the boughs, which were dusty and grey from the city's smog. It was his grandmother. Motionless, she looked up, one eye open, searching. It was too dark to see him. She seemed so small, a misplaced doll, as she swayed, squinting.

"Little Dog," she said in a whisper-shout. "You up there, Little Dog?" She craned her neck, then looked away, at the freeway in the distance. "Your mom. She not normal okay? She pain. She hurt. But she want you, she need us." She stirred in place. The leaves crackled. "She love you, Little Dog. But she sick. Sick like me. In the brains." She examined her hand, as if to make sure it still existed, then dropped it.

The boy, hearing this, pressed his lips to the cold bark to keep from crying.

She pain, the boy thought, mulling over her words. How can anyone *be* a feeling? The boy said nothing.

"You don't need to be scared, Little Dog. You smarter than me." Something crinkled. In her arms, held like a baby, was a bag of Cool Ranch Doritos. In her other hand was a Poland Spring water bottle filled with warm jasmine tea. She kept muttering to herself, "You don't need to be scared. No need."

Then she stopped and trained her eyes on him.

They watched each other between the shivered leaves. She blinked once. The branches clacked and clacked, then stopped.

Do you remember the happiest day of your life? What about the saddest? Do you ever wonder if sadness and happiness can be combined, to make a deep purple feeling, not good, not bad, but remarkable simply because you didn't have to live on one side or the other?

Main Street was empty the night Trevor and I rode our bikes down the middle of the road, our tires swallowing the fat yellow lanes as we sped. It was seven p.m., which meant there were only five hours left of Thanksgiving Day. Our breaths smoked above us. With each inhale, the pungent wood fires made a bright note in my lungs. Trevor's old man was back at the trailer, in front of the football game, eating TV dinners with bourbon and Diet Coke.

My reflection warped over the storefront glass as we rode. The stoplights blinked yellow and the only sound was the clicking spokes beneath us. We rode back and forth like that, and for a stupid moment it felt like that strip of concrete called Main Street was all we ever possessed, all that held us. Mist came down, diffracted the streetlights into huge, van Gogh orbs. Trevor, ahead of me, stood up on his bike, arms out on both sides, and shouted, "I'm flying! Hey, I'm flying!" His voice cracked as he mimicked the scene in *Titanic* where the girl stands at the bow of the ship. "I'm flying, Jack!" he shouted.

After a while Trevor stopped pedaling and let his bike slide to a stop, arms at his side.

"I'm starving."

"Me too," I said.

"There's a gas station up there." He pointed to a Shell station ahead of us. Surrounded by the vast night, it looked like a spaceship had crashed on the side of the street.

Inside, we watched two frozen egg-and-cheese sandwiches spin together in the microwave. The old white lady at the counter asked us where we were headed.

"Home," Trevor said. "My mom's stuck in traffic so just getting a snack before she comes for dinner." The woman's eyes flicked over me as she handed him the change. Trevor's mom moved to Oklahoma with her boyfriend almost five years ago.

On the stoop of a dentist's office, across the street from a shuttered Friendly's, we unwrapped our sandwiches. Warm cellophane crinkled around our hands. We chewed, stared into the restaurant windows, where a poster of a sundae advertised a ghastly green "Colossal Leprechaun Mint Boat" from last March. I held my sandwich close, letting the steam blur my vision.

"Do you think we'll still hang out when we're a hundred?" I said without thinking.

He flung the wrapper, which caught the wind and blew back atop the bush beside him. Right away I regretted asking. Swallowing, he said, "People don't live to a hundred." He ripped open a packet of ketchup, squeezed a thin red line over my sandwich.

"True." I nodded.

Then I heard the laughter. It came from a house on the street behind us.

The clear voices of children, two, maybe three, then a man's—a father? They were playing in the backyard. Not a game, exactly, but an embodiment of vague excitement, the kind known only to very young children, where delight rushes through them simply by running across an empty field not yet recognized as a tiny backyard in a shitty part of town. From their shrill cries, they were no older than six, an age where one could be ecstatic just by moving. They were little bells struck to singing, it seems, by air itself.

"That's enough. That's enough for tonight," the man said, at which the voices immediately faded. The sound of a screen door slamming. The quiet flooded back. Trevor beside me, his head in his hands.

We rode home, the streetlights here and there above us. That day was a purple day—neither good nor bad, but something we passed through. I pedaled faster, I moved, briefly unmoored. Trevor, beside me, was singing the 50 Cent song.

His voice sounded oddly young, as if it had come back from a time before I met him. As if I could turn and find a boy with a denim jacket laundered by his mom, detergent wafting up and through his hair still blond above baby-plump cheeks, training wheels rattling on the pavement.

I joined him.

"Many men, many, many, many, many men."

We sang, nearly shouting the lyrics, the wind clipping at our voices. They say a song can be a bridge, Ma. But I say it's also the ground we stand on. And maybe we sing to keep ourselves from falling. Maybe we sing to keep ourselves.

"Wish death 'pon me. Lord I don't cry no more, don't look to the sky no more. Have mercy on me."

In the blue living rooms we passed, the football game was dying down.

"Blood in my eye dawg and I can't see."

In the blue living rooms, some people won and some people lost.

In this way, autumn passed.

Inside a single-use life, there are no second chances. That's a lie but we live it. We live anyway. That's a lie but the boy opens his eyes. The room a grey-blue smear. There's music coming through the walls. Chopin, the only thing she listens to. The boy climbs out of bed and the corners of the room tilt on an axis, like a ship. But he knows this too is a trick he's making of himself. In the hallway, where the spilled lamp reveals a black mess of broken vinyl 45s, he looks for her. In her room, the covers on the bed are pulled off, the pink lace comforter piled on the floor. The night-light, only half-way in its socket, flickers and flickers. The piano drips its little notes, like rain dreaming itself whole. He makes his way to the living room. The record player by the love seat skips as it spins a record long driven to its end, the static intensifying as he approaches. But Chopin goes on, somewhere beyond reach. He follows it, head tilted for the source. And there, on the kitchen table, beside the gallon of milk on its side, the liquid coming down in white strings like a tablecloth in a nightmare, a red eye winking. The stereo she bought at Goodwill, the one that fits in her apron pocket as she works, the one she slides under her pillowcase during rainstorms, the Nocturnes growing louder after each thunder-clap. It sits in the pool of milk, as if the music was composed for it alone. In the boy's single-use body, anything's possible. So he covers the eye with his finger, to make sure he's still real, then he takes the radio. The music in his hands dripping milk, he opens the front door. It is summer. The strays beyond the railroad are barking, which means something, a rabbit or possum, has just slipped out of its life and into the world. The piano notes seep through the boy's chest as he makes his way to the backyard. Because something in him knew she'd be there. That she was waiting. Because that's what mothers do. They wait. They stand still until their children belong to someone else.

Sure enough, there she is, standing at the far end of the little chain-link yard, beside a flattened basketball, her back to him. Her shoulders are narrower than he remembers from hours ago, when she tucked him into bed, her eyes glazed and pink. Her nightgown, made from an oversized T-shirt, is torn in the back, exposing her shoulder blade, white as a halved apple. A cigarette floats to the left of her head. He walks up to her. He walks up to his mother with music in his arms, shaking. She's hunched, distorted, tiny, as if crushed by the air alone.

"I hate you," he says.

He studies her, to see what language can do—but she doesn't flinch. Only halfway turns her head. The cigarette, its ember bead, rises to her lips, then flutters near her chin.

"I don't want you to be my mom anymore." His voice strangely deeper, more full.

"You hear me? You're a monster—"

And with that her head is lopped off its shoulders.

No, she's bending over, examining something between her feet. The cigarette hangs in the air. He reaches for it. The burn he expects doesn't come. Instead, his hand crawls. Opening his palm, he discovers the firefly's severed torso, the green blood darkening on his skin. He looks up—it's just him and the radio standing beside a flat basketball in the middle of summer. The dogs now silent. And full.

"Ma," he says to no one, his eyes filling, "I didn't mean it."

"Ma!" he calls out, taking a few clipped steps. He drops the radio, it falls mouth-down in the dirt, and turns toward the house. "Ma!" He runs back inside, his hand still wet with a single-use life, looking for her.

Then I told you the truth.

It was a greyish Sunday. All morning the sky had threatened downpour. The kind of day, I had hoped, where the bond between two people might be decided on easily—the weather being so bleak we would see each other, you and I, with relief, a familiar face made more luminous than we had remembered in the backdrop of dreary light.

Inside the bright Dunkin' Donuts, two cups of black coffee steamed between us. You stared out the window. Rain slashed down the road as the cars came back from church service on Main St. "People seem to like those SUV things these days." You noted the caravan of cars at the drive-thru. "Everybody wants to sit higher and higher." Your fingers thrummed the table.

"You want sugar, Ma?" I asked. "What about cream, or actually, maybe a doughnut? Oh no, you like the croissants—"

"Say what you have to say, Little Dog." Your tone subdued, watery. The steam from the cup gave your face a shifting expression.

"I don't like girls."

I didn't want to use the Vietnamese word for it—pê-đê—from the French pédé, short for pédéraste. Before the French occupation, our Vietnamese did not have a name for queer bodies—because they were seen, like all bodies, fleshed and of one source—and I didn't want to introduce this part of me using the epithet for criminals.

You blinked a few times.

"You don't like girls," you repeated, nodding absently. I could see the words moving through you, pressing you into your chair. "Then what *do* you like? You're seventeen. You don't like anything. You don't *know* anything," you said, scratching the table.

"Boys," I said, controlling my voice. But the word felt dead in my mouth. The chair creaked as you leaned forward.

"Chocolate! I want chocolate!" A group of children in teal oversized T-shirts, just back, judging from their paper bags full of apples, from an apple-picking trip, poured into the shop, filling it with excited shrieks.

"I can leave, Ma," I offered. "If you don't want me I can go. I won't be a problem and nobody has to know. . . . Ma say something." In the cup my reflection rippled under a small black tide. "Please."

"Tell me," you said from behind the palm on your chin, "are you going to wear a dress now?"

"Ma—"

"They'll kill you," you shook your head, "you know that."

"Who will kill me?"

"They kill people for wearing dresses. It's on the news. You don't know people. You don't know them."

"I won't, Ma. I promise. Look, I never wore one before, have I? Why would I now?"

You stared at the two holes in my face. "You don't have to go anywhere. It's just you and me, Little Dog. I don't have anyone else." Your eyes were red.

The children across the shop were singing "Old MacDonald Had a Farm," their voices, their easy elation, piercing.

"Tell me," you sat up, a concerned look on your face, "when did this all start? I gave birth to a healthy, normal boy. I know that. When?"

I was six, in the first grade. The school I was at was a refurbished Lutheran church. With the kitchen forever under renovation, lunch was served in the gymnasium, the basketball court lines arcing beneath our feet as we sat at makeshift lunch tables: classroom desks bunched together in clusters. Each day the staff would wheel in huge crates filled with frozen, single-dish meals: a reddish-brown mass in a white square wrapped in cellophane. The four microwaves we lined up behind hummed throughout the lunch period as one meal after another was melted, then pinged out, blistered and steaming, into our waiting hands.

I sat down with my mush square beside a boy with a yellow polo shirt and black comb-over. His name was Gramoz and his family, I learned later, came to Hartford from Albania after the collapse of the Soviet Union. But none of that mattered that day. What mattered was that he did not have a white square with grey mush, but a sleek, turquoise lunch bag with a Velcro strap, from which he presented a tray of pizza bagels, each one the shape of over-sized jewels.

"Want one?" he said casually, biting into his.

I was too shy to touch. Gramoz, seeing this, took my hand, flipped it over, and placed one in my palm. It was heavier than I imagined. And somehow, still warm. Afterward, at recess, I followed Gramoz everywhere he went. Two rungs behind him on the monkey bars, at his heels as he climbed the ladder to the yellow swirly slide, his white Keds flashing with each step.

How else to repay the boy who gave me my first pizza bagel but to become his shadow?

The problem was that my English, at the time, was still nonexistent. I couldn't speak to him. And even if I could what could I say? Where was I following him? To what end? Perhaps it was not a destination I sought, but merely a continuation. To stay close to Gramoz was to remain within the circumference of his one act of kindness, was to go back in time, to the lunch hour, that pizza heavy in my palm.

One day, on the slide, Gramoz turned around, his cheeks puffed red, and shouted, "Stop following me, you freak! What the heck is wrong with you?" It was not the words but his eyes, squinted as if taking aim, that made me understand.

A shadow cut from its source, I stopped at the top of the slide, and watched his shiny comb-over grow smaller and smaller down the tunnel, before vanishing, without a trace, into the sound of laughing children.

When I thought it was over, that I'd done my unloading, you said, pushing your coffee aside, "Now I have something to tell *you*."

My jaw clenched. This was not supposed to be an equal exchange, not a trade. I nodded as you spoke, feigning willingness.

"You have an older brother." You swept your hair out of your eyes, unblinking. "But he's dead."

The children were still there but I no longer heard their small, perishable voices.

We were exchanging truths, I realized, which is to say, we were cutting one another.

"Look at me. You have to know this." You wore a face. Your lips a violet line.

You went on. You once had a son growing inside you, a son you had named, a name you won't repeat. The son inside you started to move, his limbs running the circumference of your belly. And you sang and spoke to him, like you did to me, told him secrets not even your husband knew. You were seventeen and back in Vietnam, the same age I was sitting across from you.

Your hands cupped now like binoculars, as if the past was something that needed to be hunted down. The table wet beneath you. You wiped it with a napkin, then kept going, telling of 1986, the year my brother, your son, appeared. How, four months into your pregnancy, when a child's face becomes a face, your husband, my father, pressured by his family, forced you to abort him.

"There was nothing to eat," you went on, your chin still cupped over the table. A man on his way to the restroom asked to get by. Without looking up, you scooted over. "People were putting sawdust in the rice to stretch it. You were lucky if you had rats to eat."

You spoke carefully, as if the story was a flame in your hands in the wind. The children were finally gone—only an elderly couple was left, two puffs of white hair behind their newspapers.

"Unlike your brother," you said, "you were not born until we knew you'd live."

Weeks after Gramoz handed me the pizza bagel, you bought me my first bicycle: a hot-pink Schwinn with training wheels and white streamers on the handgrips that rattled, like tiny pom-poms, even when I rode, as I often did, at walking speed. It was pink because that was the cheapest bike in the shop.

That afternoon, while riding in the tenement parking lot, the bike jammed to a stop. When I looked down a pair of hands were gripped on the handlebar. They belonged to a boy, maybe ten, his fat wet face wedged atop a towering, meaty torso. Before I could make out what was happening, the bike flipped backward and I landed on my butt on the pavement. You had gone upstairs to check on Lan. Stepping out from behind the boy was a smaller boy with the face of a weasel. The weasel shouted, a spray of spit rainbowed in front of him in the slanted sunlight.

The large boy took out a key chain and started scraping the paint off my bike. It came off so easily, in rosy sparks. I sat there, watching the concrete fleck with bits of pink as he gashed the key against the bike's bones. I wanted to cry but did not yet know how to in English. So I did nothing.

That was the day I learned how dangerous a color can be. That a boy could be knocked off that shade and made to reckon his trespass. Even if color is nothing but what the light reveals, that *nothing* has laws, and a boy on a pink bike must learn, above all else, the law of gravity.

That night, in the bare-bulb kitchen, I knelt beside you and watched as you painted, in long strokes that swooped, with expert precision, over the cobalt scars along the bike, the bottle of pink nail polish steady and sure in your hand.

"At the hospital, they gave me a bottle of pills. I took them for a month. To be sure. After a month, I was supposed to release it— him, I mean."

I wanted to leave, to say stop. But the price of confessing, I learned, was that you get an answer.

A month into the pills, when he should have already been gone, you felt a jab inside you. They rushed you back to the hospital, this time to the ER. "I felt him kick as they whirled me through the grey rooms, the chipped paint on the walls. The hospital still smelled of smoke and gasoline from the war."

With only Novocain injected between your thighs, the nurses went in with a long metal instrument, and just "scraped my baby out of me, like seeds from a papaya."

It was that image, its practical mundanity, the preparation of fruit I have seen you do a thousand times, the spoon gliding along the papaya's flesh-orange core, a slush of black seeds plopping into the steel sink, that made it unbearable. I pulled the hood of my white sweater over my head.

"I saw him, Little Dog. I saw my baby, just a glimpse. A brownish blur on its way to the bin."

I reached across the table and touched the side of your arm.

Just then, a Justin Timberlake song came on through the speakers, his frail falsettos woven through coffee orders, used grounds thumped against rubber trash bins. You eyed me, then past me.

When your eyes came back you said, "It was in Saigon where I heard Chopin for the first time. Did you know that?" Your Vietnamese abruptly lighter, hovering. "I must've been six or seven. The man across the street was a concert pianist trained in Paris. He would set the Steinway in his courtyard and play it in the evenings with his gate open. And his dog, this little black dog, maybe this high, would stand up and start to dance. Its little twig legs padded the dust in circles but the man would never look at the dog, but kept his eyes closed as he played. That was his power. He didn't care for the miracle he made with his hands. I sat there in the road and watched what I thought was magic: music turning an animal into a person. I looked at that dog, its ribs showing, dancing to French music and thought anything could happen. Anything." You folded your hands on the table, a mixture of sadness and agitation in the gesture. "Even when the man stopped, walked over to the dog wagging its tail, and placed the treat in the dog's open mouth, proving again that it was hunger, only hunger, not music that gave the dog its human skill, I still believed it. That anything could happen."

The rain, obedient, picked up again. I leaned back and watched it warp the windows.

Sometimes, when I'm careless, I think survival is easy: you just keep moving forward with what you have, or what's left of what you were given, until something changes—or you realize, at last, that you can change without disappearing, that all you had to do was wait until the storm passes you over and you find that—yes—your name is still attached to a living thing.

A few months before our talk at Dunkin' Donuts, a fourteen-year-old boy in rural Vietnam had acid thrown in his face after he slipped a love letter into another boy's locker. Last summer, twenty-eight-year-old Florida native Omar Mateen walked into an Orlando nightclub, raised his automatic rifle, and opened fire. Forty-nine people were killed. It was a gay club and the boys, because that's who they were—sons, teenagers—looked like me: a colored thing born of one mother, rummaging the dark, each other, for happiness.

Sometimes, when I'm careless, I believe the wound is also the place where the skin reencounters itself, asking of each end, where have you been?

Where have we been, Ma?

The weight of the average placenta is roughly one and a half pounds. A disposable organ where nutrients, hormones, and waste are passed between mother and fetus. In this way, the placenta is a kind of language—perhaps our first one, our true mother tongue. At four or five months, my brother's placenta was already fully developed. You two were speaking—in blood utterances.

"He came to me, you know."

The rain outside had stopped. The sky an emptied bowl.

"He came to you?"

"My boy, he came to me in a dream, about a week after the hospital. He was sitting on my doorstep. We watched each other for a while, then he just turned and walked away, down the alley. I think he just wanted to see what I looked like, what his mom looked like. I was a girl. Oh god . . . Oh god, I was seventeen."

In college a professor once insisted, during a digression from a lecture on *Othello,* that, to him, gay men are inherently narcissistic, and that overt narcissism might even be a sign of homosexuality in men who have not yet accepted their "tendencies." Even as I fumed in my seat, the thought wouldn't stop burrowing into me. Could it be that, all those years ago, I had followed Gramoz in the schoolyard simply because he was a boy, and therefore a mirror of myself?

But if so—why not? Maybe we look into mirrors not merely to seek beauty, regardless how illusive, but to make sure, despite the facts, that we are still here. That the hunted body we move in has not yet been annihilated, scraped out. To see yourself still *yourself* is a refuge men who have not been denied cannot know.

I read that beauty has historically demanded replication. We make more of anything we find aesthetically pleasing, whether it's a vase, a painting, a chalice, a poem. We reproduce it in order to keep it, extend it through space and time. To gaze at what pleases—a fresco, a peach-red mountain range, a boy, the mole on his jaw—is, in itself, replication—the image prolonged in the eye, making more of it, making it last. Staring into the mirror, I replicate myself into a future where I might not exist. And yes, it was not pizza bagels, all those years ago, that I wanted from Gramoz, but replication. Because his offering extended me into something worthy of generosity, and therefore seen. It was that very moreness that I wanted to prolong, to return to.

It is no accident, Ma, that the comma resembles a fetus—that curve of continuation. We were all once inside our mothers, saying, with our entire curved and silent selves, more, more, more. I want to insist that our being alive is beautiful enough to be worthy of replication. And so what? So what if all I ever made of my life was more of it?

"I have to throw up," you said.

"What?"

"I have to throw up." You rush to your feet and head to the bathroom.

"Oh my god you're serious," I said, following you. In the bathroom, you knelt at the single toilet and immediately hurled. Though your hair was tied in a bun, I knelt and, with two fingers, held your three or four strands of loose hair back in a mostly obligatory gesture. "You okay, Ma?" I spoke to the back of your head.

You hurled again, your back convulsing under my palm. Only when I saw the urinal beside your head flecked with pubic hair did I realize we were in the men's bathroom.

"I'll buy some water." I patted your back and got up.

"No," you called back, your face red, "lemonade. I need a lemonade."

We leave the Dunkin' Donuts heavier with what we know of each other. But what you didn't know was that, in fact, I *had* worn a dress before—and would do so again. That a few weeks earlier, I had danced in an old tobacco barn wearing a wine-red dress as my friend, a lanky boy with a busted eye, dizzily watched. I had salvaged the dress from your closet, the one you bought for your thirty-fifth birthday but never wore. I swirled in the sheer fabric while Trevor, perched on a stack of tires, clapped between drags on a joint, our collarbones lit sharply by a pair of cell phones placed on the floor dusted with dead moths. In that barn, for the first time in months, we weren't afraid of anybody—not even ourselves. You steer the Toyota home, me silent beside you. It seems the rain will return this evening and all night the town will be rinsed, the trees lining the freeways dripping in the metallic dark. Over dinner, I'll pull in my chair and, taking off my hood, a sprig of hay caught there from the barn weeks before will stick out from my black hair. You will reach over, brush it off, and shake your head as you take in the son you decided to keep.

The living room was miserable with laughter. On the TV the size of a microwave, a sitcom blared a tinny and fabricated glee no one believed in. No one but Trevor's dad, or rather, not so much believed, but surrendered to, chuckling in the La-Z-Boy, the bottle of Southern Comfort like a cartoon crystal in his lap. Each time he raised it, the brown drained, till only the warped colors from the TV flashed through the empty glass. He had a thick face and close-cropped pomaded hair, even at this hour. He looked like Elvis on his last day alive. The carpet under his bare feet shiny as spilled oil from years of wear.

We were behind the old man, sitting on a makeshift couch salvaged from a totaled Dodge Caravan, passing a liter of Sprite between us, giggling and texting a boy in Windsor we'd never meet. Even from here, we could smell him, strong with drink and cheap cigars, and pretended he wasn't there.

"Go ahead, laugh." Trevor's dad barely moved, but his voice

rumbled. We could feel it through the seat. "Go ahead, laugh at your father. Y'all laugh like seals."

I searched the back of his head, ringed with the chalky TV light, but saw no movement.

"We not laughing at you, man." Trevor winced and put the phone in his pocket. His hands dropped to their sides as if someone had brushed them off his knees. He glared at the back of the chair. From where we sat, only a fragment of the man's head was visible, a grab of hair and a portion of his cheek, white as sliced turkey.

"You gonna *man* me now, huh? You big, that it? You think I'm gone in my mind but I ain't, boy. I hear you. I see things." He coughed; a spray of liquor. "Don't forget I was the best seal trainer at SeaWorld. Orlando '85. Your mother was in the stands and I lifted her off her seat with my routine. My Navy Seals, them pups. I was the general of seals. That's what she called me. The general. When I told them to laugh, they laughed."

An infomercial buzzed on the set, something about an inflatable Christmas tree that you could store in your pocket. "Who the hell would want to walk around with a goddamned Christmas tree in their pocket? Tired of this country." His head rolled to one side, making a third fat roll appear on the back of his neck. "Hey—that boy with you? That China boy with you, huh? I know it. I hear him. He don't talk but I hear him." His arm shot up and I felt Trevor flinch through the couch cushion. The old man took another swig, the bottle long empty, but wiped his mouth anyway.

"Your uncle James. You 'member James right?"

"Yeah, sort of," Trevor managed.

"What's that?"

"Yes, sir."

"That's right." The old man sank further into his chair, his hair shining. The heat from his body seemed to be radiating, filling the air. "Good man, made of bone, your uncle. Bone and salt. He whooped them in that jungle. He did good for us. He burned them up. You know that, Trev? That's what it is." He went back to being motionless, his lips moved without affecting any part of his face. "He told you yet? How he burned up four of them in a ditch with gasoline? He told me that on his wedding night, can you believe it?"

I glanced at Trevor but saw only the back of his neck, his face hidden between his knees. He was aggressively tying his boots, the plastic stringheads ticking through the eyelets as his shoulders jerked.

"But it's changed now, I know that. I ain't stupid, boy. I know you hate me too. I know."

[TV laughter]

"Saw your mom two weeks ago. Gave her the keys to the storage in Windsor Locks. Don't know why took so long to get her damn furniture. Oklahoma don't look too good on that one." He paused. Took another phantom swig. "I made you fine, Trev. I know I did."

"You smell like shit." Trevor's face went stone-like.

"What's that? What I say—"

"Said you smell like shit, dude." The TV lit Trevor's face grey save for the scar on his neck, whose reddish-dark tint never changed. He got it when he was nine; his old man, in a fit of rage, shot a nail gun at the front door and the thing ricocheted. Blood so red, so everywhere, it was Christmas in June, he told me.

"You heard me." Trevor set the Sprite down on the carpet, tapped my chest, indicating we're leaving.

"You gonna talk like that now?" the old man sputtered, his eyes stuck on the screen.

"The fuck you gonna do?" Trevor said. "Go 'head, do something, make me *burn*." Trevor took a step toward the chair. He knew something I didn't. "You done?"

The old man breathed in place. The rest of the house was dark and still, like a hospital at night. After a moment he spoke, in a strange high-pitched whine. "I did good, baby." His fingers fidgeted the armrest. The people in the sitcom danced off his slick hair.

I thought I saw Trevor nod once or twice, but the TV could've been playing tricks.

"You just like James. That's right. I know. You a burner, you gonna burn them up." His voice wobbled. "See that? That's Neil Young. A legend. A warrior. You like him, Trev." He motioned toward the poster by the hall as the door closed across him, clickless. We slipped into the frosted air, walked to our bikes, the old man droning on, muffled behind us.

The pavement drifted out beneath our wheels. We said nothing as the maples, lit by sodium lamps, loomed red and windless above us. It felt good to be free of his old man's presence.

We rode along the Connecticut River as night broke into itself, the moon freshly high above the oaks, its edges hazed by an unseasonably warm autumn. The current churned with white froth to our right. Once in a while, after two or three weeks without rain, a body would float up from its depths, a bleached flash of a shoulder tapping the surface, and the families cooking out along the

banks would stop, and a hush would come down along the children, and then someone would shout, "Oh god, oh god," and someone
else would call 911. And sometimes it's a false alarm: a refrigerator
rusted and lichen-stained to the shade of a brown face. And sometimes it's the fish, gone belly-up in the thousands for no reason,
the river-face iridescent overnight.

I saw all the blocks in our city you were too busy at work to
know about, blocks where things happened. Things even Trevor, having lived all his life on this side of the river, the white side, the one I
was now riding on, never saw. I saw the lights on Asylum Ave., where
there used to be an asylum (that was actually a school for the deaf)
that caught fire and killed half a ward back in 18-something and
to this day no one knows what caused it. But I know it as the street
where my friend Sid lived with his family after they came over
from India in '95. How his mom, a schoolteacher back in New
Delhi, went door-to-door, hobbling on her bloated diabetic feet
selling hunting knives for Cutco to make ninety-seven dollars a
week—cash. There were the Canino brothers, whose father was
in jail for what seemed like two lifetimes for going seventy on a
sixty-five in front of a state trooper on 91. That and the twenty
bags of heroin and the Glock under his passenger seat. Still, still.
There was Marin, who took the bus forty-five minutes each way to
work at the Sears in Farmington, who always had gold around her
neck and ears, whose high heels clacked like the slowest, most de-
liberate applause when she walked to the corner store for cigarettes
and Hot Cheetos, her Adam's apple jutting out, a middle finger to
the men who called her *faggot,* called her *homomaphedite.* Who'd
say, holding their daughter's or son's hand, "I'm gonna kill you,

bitch, I'm gonna cut you, AIDS gonna take you out. Don't sleep tonight, don't sleep tonight, don't sleep tonight. Don't sleep."

We passed the tenement building on New Britain Ave. where we lived for three years. Where I rode my pink bike with training wheels up and down the linoleum halls so the kids on the block wouldn't beat me up for loving a pink thing. I must've ridden down those halls a hundred times a day, the little bell clinking as I hit the wall at each end. How Mr. Carlton, the man who lived in the last apartment, kept coming out and yelling at me each day, saying, "Who are you? What are you doing here? Why don't you do that outside? Who are you? You're not my daughter! You're not Destiny! Who are you?" But all that, the whole building, is gone now—replaced by a YMCA—even the tenement parking lot (where nobody parked since no one had cars), busted through with weeds nearly four feet high, is gone, all of it bulldozed and turned into a community garden with scarecrows made from mannequins thrown out by the dollar store off Bushnell. Entire families are swimming and playing handball where we used to sleep. People are doing butterfly strokes where Mr. Carlton eventually died, alone, in his bed. How no one knew for weeks until the whole floor started to reek and the SWAT team (I don't know why) had to come bust down the door with guns. How for a whole month Mr. Carlton's things were left out in a big iron dumpster out back, and a wooden hand-painted pony, its tongue-lolled face, peeked out of the dumpster's top in the rain.

Trevor and I kept riding, past Church St. where Big Joe's sister OD'd, then the parking lot behind the MEGA XXXLOVE DE-

POT where Sasha OD'd, the park where Jake and B-Rab OD'd. Except B-Rab lived, only to be caught, years later, stealing laptops from Trinity College and got four years in county—no parole. Which was heavy, *especially* for a white kid from the suburbs. There was Nacho, who lost his right leg in the Gulf War and whom you could find on weekends sliding under jack-raised cars with a skateboard at the Maybelle Auto Repair where he worked. Where he once pulled a beautiful screaming red-faced baby from the trunk of a Nissan left in the back of the shop during a blizzard. How he let his crutches fall and cradled the baby with both hands and the air held him up for the first time in years as the snow came down, then rose back up from the ground so bright that, for a blurred merciful hour, everyone in the city forgot why they were trying to get out of it.

There's Mozzicato's on Franklin, where I had my first cannoli. Where nothing I knew ever died. Where I sat looking out the window one summer night from the fifth floor of our building, and the air was warm and sweet like it is now, and there were the low voices of young couples, their Converses and Air Force Ones tapping against each other on the fire escapes as they worked to make the body speak its other tongues, the sound of matches, or flames sparked from lighters the shape and shine of 9mms or Colt .45s, which was how we turned death into a joke, how we reduced fire to the size of cartoon raindrops, then sucked them through cigarillo tips, like myths. Because eventually the river rises here. It overflows to claim it all and to show us what we lost, like it always had.

The bike spokes whirred. The smell of sewage from the water plant stung my eyes just before the wind did with it what it does with the names of the dead, swept it behind me.

We crossed it, we left it all behind, the spokes ticking us deeper toward the suburbs. When we hit the pavement in East Hartford, the scent of wood smoke blown from the hills came down and cleared the mind. I stared at Trevor's back as we rode, his brown UPS jacket, the one his daddy got from working there a week before getting fired after downing a six-pack on his break and waking up near midnight in a pile of cardboard boxes, now purplish under the moon.

We made our way down Main Street. When we came upon the Coca-Cola bottling plant, its neon sign burning huge above the building, Trevor shouted, "Fuck Coca-Cola! Sprite for life, motherfucker!" He glanced back and laughed brokenly. "Yeah, fuck them," I offered. But he didn't hear.

The streetlights fell away and the sidewalk led up to a grassy shoulder, which meant we're heading up the hills, to the mansions. Soon we were deep in the burbs, in South Glastonbury, and the house lights started appearing, first as orange sparks flitting through the trees, but as we got closer, they grew into wide, fat sheets of gold. You could peer through these windows, windows free of steel bars, their curtains drawn wide open. Even from the street you could see the sparkling chandeliers, dining tables, multicolored Tiffany lamps shaded with decorative glass. The houses were so large you could look in all the windows and never see a single person.

As we climbed the road up the steep hill, the starless sky opened up, the trees fell slowly back, and the houses grew further and further apart from one another. One set of neighbors was separated by an entire orchard, whose apples had already begun to rot across the fields, no one to pick them. The fruit rolled into the street where their flesh burst, pulped and browned, under the passing cars.

We stopped at the top of one of the hills, exhausted. Moonlight appraised the orchard to our right. The apples glowed dimly on their branches, dropping here and there in quick thuds, their sweet fermented stink in our lungs. Deep in the oaks across the road, invisible tree frogs let out their rasped calls. We let our bikes drop and sat on a wooden fence along the road. Trevor lit a cigarette, drew from it, eyes closed, then passed the ruby bead toward my fingers. I sucked but coughed, my spit thick from the ride. The smoke warmed my lungs and my eyes settled on a cluster of mansions in the small valley before us.

"They say Ray Allen lives up here," Trevor said.

"The basketball player, right?"

"He played for UConn—dude probably has *two* cribs up here."

"Maybe he lives in that one," I said, pointing the cigarette to the only darkened house at the edge of the valley. The house was almost invisible but for the white trim around its edges, like the skeleton of a prehistoric creature. Maybe Ray Allen is away, I thought, playing in the NBA and too busy to live in it. I passed the cigarette back.

"If Ray Allen was my dad," he said, his gaze still fixed on the bone house, "that'd be my house and you could always come and crash there."

"You already have a dad."

He flicked the roach on the road and looked away. It fell and broke into an orange gash on the pavement, then sputtered out.

"Forget that guy, little man," Trevor looked at me, soft, "he's not worth it."

"Worth what?"

"Getting pissed over, dude. Ah—score!" He took out a mini Snickers from his coat pocket. "Must've been here since last Halloween."

"Who said I was?"

"He just got his things, you know?" He pointed the Snickers to his head. "The drink gets to him."

"Yeah. I guess." The tree frogs seemed further away, smaller. Some kind of quiet sharpened between us.

"Hey, don't do the fuckin' silent thing, man. It's a fag move. I mean—" A frustrated sigh escaped him. He bit into the Snickers. "Want half?"

By way of reply I opened my mouth. He placed the thumb-sized morsel on my tongue, wiped his lips with his wrist, and looked away.

"Let's get out of here," I said, chewing.

He was about to say something else, his teeth grey pills in the moonlight, then got up and stumbled toward his bike. I picked up my own, the steel already wet with dew, and that's when I saw it. Actually, Trevor saw it first, letting out an almost imperceptible gasp. I turned around and we both just stood there leaning against our bikes.

It was Hartford. It was a cluster of light that pulsed with a force I never realized it possessed. Maybe it was because his breaths were so clear to me then, how I imagined the oxygen in his throat, his lungs, the bronchi and blood vessels expanding, how it moved through all the places I'll never see, that I keep returning to this most basic measurement of life, even long after he's gone.

But for now, the city brims before us with a strange, rare brilliance—as if it was not a city at all, but the sparks made by some god sharpening his weapons above us.

"Fuck," Trevor whispered. He put his hands in his pockets and spat on the ground.

"Fuck."

The city throbbed, shimmered. Then, trying to snap himself out of it, he said, "Fuck Coca-Cola."

"Yeah, Sprite for life, fuckers," I added, not knowing then what I know now: that Coca-Cola and Sprite were made by the same damn company. That no matter who you are or what you love or where you stand, it was always Coca-Cola in the end.

Trevor rusted pickup and no license.

Trevor sixteen; blue jeans streaked with deer blood.

Trevor too fast and not enough.

Trevor waving his John Deere cap from the driveway as you ride by on your squeaky Schwinn.

Trevor who fingered a freshman girl then tossed her underwear in the lake *for fun.*

For summer. For your hands

were wet and Trevor's a name like an engine starting up in the night. Who snuck out to meet a boy like you. Yellow and barely there. Trevor going fifty through his daddy's wheat field. Who jams all his fries into a Whopper and chews with both feet on the gas. Your eyes closed, riding shotgun, the wheat a yellow confetti.

Three freckles on his nose.

Three periods to a boy-sentence.

Trevor Burger King over McDonald's 'cause the smell of smoke on the beef *makes it real.*

Trevor bucktooth clicking on his inhaler as he sucked, eyes shut.

Trevor *I like sunflowers best. They go so high.*

Trevor with the scar like a comma on his neck, syntax of what next what next what next.

Imagine going so high and still opening that big.

Trevor loading the shotgun two red shells at a time.

It's kind of like being brave, I think. Like you got this big ole head full of seeds and no arms to defend yourself.

His hard lean arms aimed in the rain.

He touches the trigger's black tongue and you swear you taste his finger in your mouth as it pulls. Trevor pointing at the one-winged sparrow thrashing in black dirt and takes it

for something new. Something smoldering like a word. Like a Trevor

who knocked on your window at three in the morning, who you thought was smiling until you saw the blade held over his mouth. *I made this, I made this for you,* he said, the knife suddenly in your hand. Trevor later

on your steps in the grey dawn. His face in his arms. *I don't wanna,* he said. His panting. His shaking hair. The blur of it. *Please tell me I am not,* he said through the sound of his knuckles as he popped them like the word *But But But.* And you take a step back. *Please tell me I am not,* he said, *I am not*

a faggot. Am I? Am I? Are you?

Trevor the hunter. Trevor the carnivore, the redneck, not

a pansy, shotgunner, sharpshooter, not fruit or fairy. Trevor meateater but not

veal. *Never veal. Fuck that, never again* after his daddy told him the story when he was seven, at the table, veal roasted with rosemary. How they were made. How the difference between veal and beef is the children. The veal are the children of cows, are calves. They are locked in boxes the size of themselves. A body-box, like a coffin, but alive, like a home. The children, the veal, they stand very still because tenderness depends on how little the world touches you. To stay tender, the weight of your life cannot lean on your bones.

We love eatin' what's soft, his father said, looking dead

into Trevor's eyes. Trevor who would never eat a child. Trevor the child with the scar on his neck like a comma. A comma you now

put your mouth to. That violet hook holding two complete thoughts, two complete bodies without subjects. Only verbs. When you say *Trevor* you mean the action, the pine-stuck thumb on the Bic lighter, the sound of his boots

on the Chevy's sun-bleached hood. The wet live thing dragged into the truck bed behind him.

Your Trevor, your brunette but blond-dusted-arms *man* pulling you into the truck. When you say *Trevor* you mean you are the hunted, a hurt he can't refuse because *that's something, baby. That's real.*

And you wanted to be real, to be swallowed by what drowns you only to surface, brimming at the mouth. Which is kissing.

Which is nothing

if you forget.

His tongue in your throat, Trevor speaks for you. He speaks and you darken, a flashlight going out in his hands so he knocks you in the head to keep the bright on. He turns you this way and that to find his path through the dark woods.

The dark words—

which have limits, like bodies. Like the calf

waiting in its coffin-house. No window—but a slot for oxygen. Pink nose pressed to the autumn night, inhaling. The bleached stench of cut grass, the tar and gravel road, coarse sweetness of leaves in a bonfire, the minutes, the distance, the earthly manure of his mother a field away.

Clover. Sassafras. Douglas fir. Scottish myrtle.

The boy. The motor oil. The body, it fills up. And your thirst over-flows what holds it. And your ruin, you thought it would nourish him. That he would feast on it and grow into a beast you could hide in.

But every box will be opened in time, in language. The line broken,

like Trevor, who stared too long into your face, saying, *Where am I? Where am I?*

Because by then there was blood in your mouth.

By then the truck was totaled into a dusked oak, smoke from the hood. Trevor, vodka-breathed and skull-thin, said, *It feels good.* Said, *Don't go nowhere*

as the sun slid into the trees. *Don't this feel good?* as the windows reddened like someone seeing through shut eyes.

Trevor who texted you after two months of silence—

writing *please* instead of *plz.*

Trevor who was running from home, his crazy old man. *Who was getting the fuck out.* Soaked Levi's. Who ran away to the park because where else when you're sixteen.

Who you found in the rain, under the metal slide shaped like a hippopotamus. Whose icy boots you took off and covered, one by one, each dirt-cold toe, with your mouth. The way your mother used to do when you were small and shivering.

Because he was shivering. Your Trevor. Your all-American beef but no veal. Your John Deere. Jade vein in his jaw: stilled lightning you trace with your teeth.

Because he tasted like the river and maybe you were one wing away from sinking.

Because the calf waits in its cage so calmly

to be veal.

Because you remembered

and memory is a second chance.

Both of you lying beneath the slide: two commas with no words, at last, to keep you apart.

You who crawled from the wreck of summer like sons leaving their mothers' bodies.

A calf in a box, waiting. A box tighter than a womb. The rain coming down, its hammers on the metal like an engine revving up. The night standing in violet air, a calf

shuffling inside, hoofs soft as erasers, the bell on its neck ringing

and ringing. The shadow of a man growing up to it. The man with his keys, the commas of doors. Your head on Trevor's chest. The calf being led by a string, how it stops

to inhale, nose pulsing with dizzying sassafras. Trevor asleep

beside you. Steady breaths. Rain. Warmth welling through his plaid shirt like steam issuing from the calf's flanks as you listen to the bell across the star-flooded field, the sound shining

like a knife. The sound buried deep in Trevor's chest and you listen.

That ringing. You listen like an animal

learning how to speak.

III

I'm on the train from New York City. In the window my face won't let me go, it hovers above windswept towns as the Amtrak slashes past lots stacked with shelled cars and farm tractors shot through with rust, backyards and their repeating piles of rotted firewood, the oily mounds gone mushy, pushed through the crisscross of chain-link fences, then hardened in place. Past warehouse after warehouse graffitied, then painted white, then graffitied again, the windows smashed out for so long glass no longer litters the ground below, windows you can look through, and glimpse, beyond the empty dark inside, the sky, where a wall used to be. And there, just beyond Bridgeport, sits the one boarded house in the middle of a parking lot the size of two footballs fields, the yellow lines running right up to the battered porch.

The train barrels past them all, these towns I have come to know only by what leaves them, myself included. The light on the Connecticut River is the brightest thing in the afternoon's overcast. I'm on this train 'cause I'm going back to Hartford.

I take out my phone. And a barrage of texts floods the screen, just like I expected.

> u hear abt trev?
>
> check fb
>
> it's about Trevor pick up
>
> fuck this si horrifc call me if u want
>
> I just saw. damn
>
> i'll call ashley to make sure
>
> just lmk ur good
>
> the wakes on sunday
>
> its trev this time? I knew it

For no reason, I text him: *Trevor I'm sorry come back,* then turn off the phone, terrified he'd answer.

It's already night by the time I get off at Hartford's Union Station. I stand in the greasy parking lot as people hurry through the drizzle into waiting taxis. It's been five years and three months since Trevor and I first met, since the barn, the Patriots game through radio static, the army helmet on the dusty floor. I wait alone under an awning for the bus that will take me across the river, to the town that holds everything Trevor except Trevor himself.

I did not tell anyone I was coming. I was in the Italian American Lit class at a city college in Brooklyn when I saw, on my phone, a Facebook update from Trevor's account, posted by his old man.

Trevor had passed away the night before. *I'm broken in two,* the message said. In two, it was the only thought I could keep, sitting in my seat, how losing a person could make more of us, the living, make us two.

I picked up my bag and left the class. The professor, discussing a passage from Pietro di Donato's *Christ in Concrete,* stopped, looked at me, waiting for an explanation. When I gave none she continued, her voice trailing behind me as I fled the building. I walked all the way uptown, along the East Side, following the 6 train up to Grand Central.

Into—yes, that's more like it. As in, *Now I'm broken into.*

The bus's lights make it feel like a dentist's office gliding through the wet streets. A woman behind me coughs fitfully between bursts of Haitian-inflected French. There's a man next to her—husband, brother?—who rarely speaks save for the occasional "Uh-huh" or "Bien, bien." On the highway, the October trees blur by, branches raking purple sky. In between them, the lampposts of soundless towns hang in fog. We cross a bridge and a roadside gas station leaves a neon throb in my head.

When the dark in the bus returns, I look down at my lap and hear his voice. *You should stay.* I glance up and see the fabric peeling from the top of his truck, the yellow foam spilling out at the tear, and I'm back in the passenger seat. It's mid-August and we're parked outside the Town Line Diner in Wethersfield. The air around us dark red, or perhaps that's how all evenings, rendered in my memory of him, appear. Bludgeoned.

"You should stay," he says, gazing out across the lot, his face smeared with motor oil from his shift at the Pennzoil in Hebron. But we both know I'm leaving. I'm going to New York, to college. The whole point of us meeting was to say goodbye, or rather, just to be side by side, a farewell of presence, of proximity, the way men are supposed to do.

We were to go to the diner for waffles, "for old times' sake," he said, but when we get there, neither of us moves. Inside the diner, a trucker sits alone over a plate of eggs. On the other side, a middle-aged couple is tucked into a booth, laughing, their arms animated over their oversized sandwiches. A single waitress hovers between the two tables. When the rain starts, the glass warps them, so that only their shades, colors, like impressionist paintings, remain.

"Don't be scared," his voice says. He stares at the people glowing in the diner. The tenderness in his tone holds me to the seat, the washed-out town. "You're smart," he says. "You're gonna kill it in New York." His voice sounds unfinished. And that's when I realize he's high. That's when I see the bruises along his upper arms, the veins bulged and blackened where the needles foraged.

"Okay," I say as the waitress gets up to warm up the trucker's coffee. "Okay, Trevor," as if agreeing to a task.

"They're old as fuck and they're still trying." He almost laughs.

"Who?" I turn to him.

"That married couple. They're still trying to be happy." He is slurring, eyes grey as sink water. "It's raining like hell and they out there eating soggy Reubens trying to get it right." He spits into the empty cup and lets out a short, exhausted chuckle. "I bet they've been eating the same sandwiches forever."

I smile, for no reason.

He falls back in the seat, lets his head roll to one side, and eases out a come-on grin. He starts to fumble the buckle over his Levi's.

"Come on, Trev. You're blazed. Let's not, okay?"

"I used to hate it when you call me Trev." He drops his hands, they lie in his lap like unearthed roots. "You think I'm fucked up?"

"No," I mumble, turning away. I press my forehead against the window, where my reflection hovers above the parking lot, the rain falling through it. "I think you're just you."

I didn't know that would be the last time I'd see him, his neck scar lit blue by the diner's neon marquee. To see that little comma again, to put my mouth there, let my shadow widen the scar until, at last, there was no scar to be seen at all, just a vast and equal dark sealed by my lips. A comma superimposed by a period the mouth so naturally makes. Isn't that the saddest thing in the world, Ma? A comma forced to be a period?

"Hello," he says, without turning his head. We had decided, shortly after we met, because our friends were already dying from overdoses, to never tell each other goodbye or good night.

"Hello, Trevor," I say into the back of my wrist, keeping it in. The engine jolts, stutters up, behind me the woman coughs. I'm back inside the bus again, staring at the blue mesh seat in front of me.

I get off on Main St. and immediately head toward Trevor's house. I move as if I'm late to myself, as if I'm catching up. But Trevor is no longer a destination.

Realizing, too late, that it's useless to show up unannounced at a dead boy's house to be greeted only by his grief-fucked father, I keep walking. I reach the corner of Harris and Magnolia, where I turn, out of habit or possession, into the park, cross the three baseball fields, the earth rising up musty and fresh beneath my boots. Rain in my hair, down my face, shirt collar. I hurry toward the street on the other side of the park, follow it down to the cul-de-sac, where the house sits, so grey the rain almost claims it, rubbing its edges into weather.

At the front steps, I take the keys from my bag and jostle the door open. It's nearly midnight. The house sends over me a sheet of warmth, mixed with the sweet musk of old clothes. Everything quiet. The living room TV hums on mute, its blue washes over the empty couch, a half-eaten bag of peanuts on the seat. I shut off the TV, walk up the stairs, turn toward the room. The door's ajar, revealing the glow of a clamshell night-light. I push it open. You're lying, not on your bed, but on the floor, on a mat made of folded blankets. Your work at the nail salon has left your back so badly strained the bed has gotten too soft to hold your joints in place through a night's sleep.

I crawl next to you on the mat. Rain, collected in my hair, falls and blotches your white sheets. I lie down, facing the bed, my back to your back. You startle awake.

"What? What are you doing? My god, you're wet . . . your clothes, Little Dog . . . what? What's going on?" You sit up, pull my face to you. "What happened to you?" I shake my head, smile stupidly.

You search me for answers, for cuts, feeling my pockets, under my shirt.

Slowly, you lie down on your side. The space between us thin and cold as a windowpane. I turn away—even if what I want most is to tell you everything.

It's in these moments, next to you, that I envy words for doing what we can never do—how they can tell all of themselves simply by standing still, simply by *being*. Imagine I could lie down beside you and my whole body, every cell, radiates a clear, singular meaning, not so much a writer as a word pressed down beside you.

There's a word Trevor once told me about, one he learned from Buford, who served in the navy in Hawaii during the Korean War: kipuka. The piece of land that's spared after a lava flow runs down the slope of a hill—an island formed from what survives the smallest apocalypse. Before the lava descended, scorching the moss along the hill, that piece of land was insignificant, just another scrap in an endless mass of green. Only by enduring does it earn its name. Lying on the mat with you, I cannot help but want us to be our own kipuka, our own aftermath, visible. But I know better.

You place a sticky hand on my neck: lavender lotion. Rain drums the gutters along the house. "What is it, Little Dog? You can tell me. Come on, you're making me scared."

"I hate him, Ma," I whisper in English, knowing the words seal you off from me. "I hate him. I hate him." And I start to cry.

"Please, I don't know what you're saying. What is that?"

I reach back, clutching two of your fingers, and press my face into the dark slot under the bed. On the far end, near the wall, too far for anyone to reach, beside an empty water bottle, a single sock crumpled and filmed with dust. Hello.

ear Ma—

Let me begin again.

I am writing because it's late.

Because it's 9:52 p.m. on a Tuesday and you must be walking home after the closing shift.

I'm not with you 'cause I'm at war. Which is one way of saying it's already February and the president wants to deport my friends. It's hard to explain.

For the first time in a long time, I'm trying to believe in heaven, in a place we can be together after all this blows ~~over~~ up.

They say every snowflake is different—but the blizzard, it covers us all the same. A friend in Norway told me a story about a painter who went out during a storm, searching for the right shade of green, and never returned.

I'm writing you because I'm not the one leaving, but the one coming back, empty-handed.

You once asked me what it means to be a writer. So here goes.

Seven of my friends are dead. Four from overdoses. Five, if you count Xavier who flipped his Nissan doing ninety on a bad batch of fentanyl.

I don't celebrate my birthday anymore.

Take the long way home with me. Take the left on Walnut, where you'll see the Boston Market where I worked for a year when I was seventeen (after the tobacco farm). Where the Evangelical boss—the one with nose pores so large, biscuit crumbs from his lunch would get lodged in them—never gave us any breaks. Hungry on a seven-hour shift, I'd lock myself in the broom closet and stuff my mouth with cornbread I snuck in my black, standard-issue apron.

Trevor was put on OxyContin after breaking his ankle doing dirt bike jumps in the woods a year before I met him. He was fifteen.

OxyContin, first mass-produced by Purdue Pharma in 1996, is an opioid, essentially making it heroin in pill form.

I never wanted to build a "body of work," but to preserve these, our bodies, breathing and unaccounted for, inside the work.

Take it or leave it. The body, I mean.

Take a left on Harris St., where all that's left of the house that burned down that summer during a thunderstorm is a chain-linked dirt lot.

The truest ruins are not written down. The girl Grandma knew back in Go Cong, the one whose sandals were cut from the tires of a burned-out army jeep, who was erased by an air strike three weeks before the war ended—she's a ruin no one can point to. A ruin without location, like a language.

After a month on the Oxy, Trevor's ankle healed, but he was a full-blown addict.

In a world myriad as ours, the gaze is a singular act: to look at something is to fill your whole life with it, if only briefly. Once, after my fourteenth birthday, crouched between the seats of an abandoned school bus in the woods, I filled my life with a line of cocaine. A white letter "I" glowed on the seat's peeling leather. Inside me the "I" became a switchblade—and something tore. My stomach forced up but it was too late. In minutes, I became more of myself. Which is to say the monstrous part of me got so large, so familiar, I could want it. I could kiss it.

The truth is none of us are enough enough. But you know this already.

The truth is I came here hoping for a reason to stay.

Sometimes those reasons are small: the way you pronounce spaghetti as "bahgeddy."

It's late in the season—which means the winter roses, in full bloom along the national bank, are suicide notes.

Write that down.

They say nothing lasts forever but they're just scared it will last longer than they can love it.

Are you there? Are you still walking?

They say nothing lasts forever and I'm writing you in the voice of an endangered species.

The truth is I'm worried they will get us before they *get us*.

Tell me where it hurts. You have my word.

Back in Hartford, I used to wander the streets at night by my-self. Sleepless, I'd get dressed, climb through the window—and just walk.

Some nights I would hear an animal shuffling, unseen, behind garbage bags, or the wind unexpectedly strong overhead, a rush of leaves clicking down, the scrape of branches from a maple out of sight. But mostly, there were only my footsteps on the pavement steaming with fresh rain, the scent of decade-old tar, or the dirt on a baseball field under a few stars, the gentle brush of grass on the soles of my Vans on a highway median.

But one night I heard something else.

Through the lightless window of a street-level apartment, a man's voice in Arabic. I recognized the word *Allah*. I knew it was a prayer by the tone he used to lift it, as if the tongue was the smallest arm from which a word like that could be offered. I imagined it floating above his head as I sat there on the curb, waiting for the soft clink I knew was coming. I wanted the word to fall, like a screw in a guillotine, but it didn't. His voice, it went higher and higher, and my hands, they grew pinker with each inflection. I watched my skin intensify until, at last, I looked up—and it was dawn. It was over. I was blazed in the blood of light.

Salat al-fajr: a prayer before sunrise. "Whoever prays the dawn prayer in congregation," said the Prophet Muhammad, "it is as if he had prayed the whole night long."

I want to believe, walking those aimless nights, that I was praying. For what I'm still not sure. But I always felt it was just ahead of me. That if I walked far enough, long enough, I would find it—perhaps even hold it up, like a tongue at the end of its word.

First developed as a painkiller for cancer patients undergoing chemotherapy, OxyContin, along with its generic forms, was soon prescribed for all bodily pain: arthritis, muscle spasms, and migraines.

Trevor was into *The Shawshank Redemption* and Jolly Ranchers, Call of Duty and his one-eyed border collie, Mandy. Trevor who, after an asthma attack, said, hunched over and gasping, "I think I just deep-throated an invisible cock," and we both cracked up like it wasn't December and we weren't under an overpass waiting out the rain on the way home from the needle exchange. Trevor was a boy who had a name, who wanted to go to community college to study physical therapy. Trevor was alone in his room when he died, surrounded by posters of Led Zeppelin. Trevor was twenty-two. Trevor was.

The official cause of death, I would learn later, was an overdose from heroin laced with fentanyl.

Once, at a writing conference, a white man asked me if destruction was necessary for art. His question was genuine. He leaned forward, his blue gaze twitching under his cap stitched gold with *'Nam Vet 4 Life,* the oxygen tank connected to his nose hissing beside him. I regarded him the way I do every white veteran from that war, thinking he could be my grandfather, and I said no. "No, sir, destruction is not necessary for art." I said that, not because I was certain, but because I thought my saying it would help me believe it.

But why can't the language for creativity be the language of regencration?

You killed that poem, we say. You're a killer. You came in to that novel guns blazing. I am hammering this paragraph, I am banging them out, we say. I owned that workshop. I shut it down. I crushed them. We smashed the competition. I'm wrestling with the muse. The state, where people live, is a battleground state. The audience a target audience. "Good for you, man," a man once said to me at a party, "you're making a killing with poetry. You're knockin' 'em dead."

One afternoon, while watching TV with Lan, we saw a herd of buffalo run, single file, off a cliff, a whole steaming row of them thundering off the mountain in Technicolor. "Why they die themselves like that?" she asked, mouth open. Like usual, I made something up on the spot: "They don't mean to, Grandma. They're just following their family. That's all. They don't know it's a cliff."

"Maybe they should have a stop sign then."

We had many stop signs on our block. They weren't always there. There was this woman named Marsha down the street. She was overweight and had hair like a rancher's widow, a kind of mullet cut with thick bangs. She would go door-to-door, hobbling on her bad leg, gathering signatures for a petition to put up stop signs in the neighborhood. She has two boys herself, she told you at the door, and she wants all the kids to be safe when they play.

Her sons were Kevin and Kyle. Kevin, two years older than me, overdosed on heroin. Five years later, Kyle, the younger one, also overdosed. After that Marsha moved to a mobile park in Coventry with her sister. The stop signs remain.

The truth is we don't have to die if we don't feel like it.

Just kidding.

Do you remember the morning, after a night of snow, when we found the letters *FAG4LIFE* scrawled in red spray paint across our front door?

The icicles caught the light and everything looked nice and about to break.

"What does it mean?" you asked, coatless and shivering. "It says 'Merry Christmas,' Ma," I said, pointing. "See? That's why it's red. For luck."

They say addiction might be linked to bipolar disorder. It's the chemicals in our brains, they say. I got the wrong chemicals, Ma. Or rather, I don't get enough of one or the other. They have a pill for it. They have an industry. They make millions. Did you know people get rich off of sadness? I want to meet the millionaire of American sadness. I want to look him in the eye, shake his hand, and say, "It's been an honor to serve my country."

The thing is, I don't want my sadness to be othered from me just as I don't want my happiness to be othered. They're both mine. I made them, dammit. What if the elation I feel is not another "bipolar episode" but something I fought hard for? Maybe I jump up and down and kiss you too hard on the neck when I learn, upon coming home, that it's pizza night because sometimes pizza night is more than enough, is my most faithful and feeble beacon. What if I'm running outside because the moon tonight is children's-book huge and *ridiculous* over the line of pines, the sight of it a strange sphere of medicine?

It's like when all you've been seeing before you is a cliff and then this bright bridge appears out of nowhere, and you run fast across it knowing, sooner or later, there'll be yet another cliff on the other side. What if my sadness is actually my most brutal teacher? And the lesson is always this: You don't have to be like the buffaloes. You can stop.

There was a war, the man on TV said, but it's "lowered" now.

Yay, I think, swallowing my pills.

The truth is my recklessness is body-width.

Once, the anklebone of a blond boy underwater.

There was a greenish light in that line and you saw it.

The truth is we can survive our lives, but not our skin. But you know this already.

I never did heroin because I'm chicken about needles. When I declined his offer to shoot it, Trevor, tightening the cell phone charger around his arm with his teeth, nodded toward my feet. "Looks like you dropped your tampon." Then he winked, smiled—and faded back into the dream he made of himself.

Using a multimillion-dollar ad campaign, Purdue sold OxyContin to doctors as a safe, "abuse-resistant" means of managing pain. The company went on to claim that less than one percent of users became addicted, which was a lie. By 2002, prescriptions of Oxy-

Contin for noncancer pain increased nearly ten times, with total sales reaching over $3 billion.

What if art was not measured by quantity but ricochets?

What if art was not measured?

The one good thing about national anthems is that we're already on our feet, and therefore ready to run.

The truth is one nation, under drugs, under drones.

The first time I saw a man naked he seemed forever.

He was my father, undressing after work. I am trying to end the memory. But the thing about forever is you can't take it back.

Let me stay here until the end, I said to the lord, and we'll call it even.

Let me tie my shadow to your feet and call it friendship, I said to myself.

I woke to the sound of wings in the room, as if a pigeon had flown through the opened window and was now thrashing against the ceiling. I switched on the lamp. As my eyes adjusted, I saw Trevor sprawled on the floor, his sneaker kicking against the dresser as he rippled under the seizure. We were in his basement. We were in a war. I held his head, foam from his lips spreading down my arm, and screamed for his old man. That night, in the hospital, he lived. It was already the second time.

Horror story: hearing Trevor's voice when I close my eyes one night four years after he died.

He's singing "This Little Light of Mine" again, the way he used to sing it—abrupt, between lulls in our conversations, his arm hanging out the window of the Chevy, tapping the beat on the faded red exterior. I lay there in the dark, mouthing the words till he appears again—young and warm and enough.

The black wren this morning on my windowsill: a charred pear.

That meant nothing but you have it now.

Take a right, Ma. There's the lot behind the bait and tackle shack where one summer I watched Trevor skin a raccoon he shot with Buford's Smith & Wesson. He grimaced as he worked the thing out of itself, his teeth green from the drugs, like glow-in-the-dark stars in daylight. On the truck bed the black pelt rippled in the breeze. A few feet away, a pair of eyes, grained with dirt, stunned by the vision of their new gods.

Can you hear it, the wind driving the river behind the Episcopal church on Wyllys St.?

The closest I've ever come to god was the calm that filled me after orgasm. That night, as Trevor slept beside me, I kept seeing the raccoon's pupils, how they couldn't shut without the skull. I'd like to think, even without ourselves, that we could still see. I'd like to think we'd never close.

You and I, we were Americans until we opened our eyes.

Are you cold? Don't you think it's strange that to warm yourself is to basically touch the body with the temperature of its marrow?

They will want you to succeed, but never more than them. They will write their names on your leash and call you *necessary*, call you *urgent*.

From the wind, I learned a syntax for forwardness, how to move through obstacles by wrapping myself around them. You can make it home this way. Believe me, you can shake the wheat and still be nameless as cokedust on the tender side of a farm-boy's fist.

How come each time my hands hurt me, they become more mine?

Go past the cemetery on House St. The one with headstones so worn the names resemble bite marks. The oldest grave holds a Mary-Anne Cowder (1784–1784).

After all, we are here only once.

Three weeks after Trevor died a trio of tulips in an earthenware pot stopped me in the middle of my mind. I had woken abruptly and, still dazed from sleep, mistook the dawn light hitting the petals for the flowers emitting their own luminescence. I crawled to the glowing cups, thinking I was seeing a miracle, my own burning bush. But when I got closer, my head blocked the rays and the tulips turned off. This also means nothing, I know. But some nothings change everything after them.

In Vietnamese, the word for missing someone and remembering them is the same: nhớ. Sometimes, when you ask me over the phone, *Con nhớ mẹ không?* I flinch, thinking you meant, *Do you remember me?*

I miss you more than I remember you.

They will tell you that to be political is to be *merely* angry, and therefore artless, depthless, "raw," and empty. They will speak of the political with embarrassment, as if speaking of Santa Claus or the Easter Bunny.

They will tell you that great writing "breaks free" from the political, thereby "transcending" the barriers of difference, uniting people toward universal truths. They'll say this is achieved through *craft* above all. Let's see how it's made, they'll say—as if how something is assembled is alien to the impulse that created it. As if the first chair was hammered into existence without considering the human form.

I know. It's not fair that the word *laughter* is trapped inside *slaughter*.

We'll have to cut it open, you and I, like a newborn lifted, red and trembling, from the just-shot doe.

Cocaine, laced with oxycodone, makes everything fast and still at once, like when you're on the train and, gazing across the fogged New England fields, at the brick Colt factory where cousin Victor works, you see its blackened smokestack—parallel to the train, like it's following you, like where you're from won't let you off the hook. Too much joy, I swear, is lost in our desperation to keep it.

After riding our bikes for two hours one night so Trevor could score on the outskirts of Windsor, we sat on the swings across from the hippopotamus slide in the elementary school playscape, the rubber cold beneath us. He had just shot up. I watched as he held a flame under the plastic transdermal adhesive until the fentanyl bubbled and gathered into a sticky tar at the center. When the plastic warped at the edges, browning, he stopped, took the needle, and sucked the clear liquid past the black ticks on the cylinder.

His sneakers grazed the woodchips. In the dark the purple hippo, its mouth open where you can crawl through, looked like a wrecked car. "Hey, Little Dog." From his slur, I could tell that his eyes were closed.

"Yeah?"

"Is it true though?" His swing kept creaking. "You think you'll be really gay, like, forever? I mean," the swing stopped, "I think me . . . I'll be good in a few years, you know?"

I couldn't tell if by "really" he meant *very gay* or *truly gay*.

"I think so," I said, not knowing what I meant.

"That's crazy." He laughed, the fake one you use to test the thickness of a silence. His shoulders wilted, the drug running through him steady.

Then something brushed my mouth. Startled, I clenched around it anyway. Trevor had slipped a bogie between my lips, lit it. The flame flashed in his eyes, glazed and bloodshot. I swallowed the sweet scalding smoke, fighting back tears—and winning. I considered the stars, the smattering of blue-white phosphorescence, and wondered how anyone could call the night dark.

———

Round the corner by the traffic light blinking yellow. Because that's what the lights do in our town after midnight—they forget why they're here.

You asked me what it's like to be a writer and I'm giving you a mess, I know. But it's a mess, Ma—I'm not making this up. I made it down. That's what writing is, after all the nonsense, getting down so low the world offers a merciful new angle, a larger vision made of small things, the lint suddenly a huge sheet of fog exactly the size of your eyeball. And you look through it and see the thick steam in the all-night bathhouse in Flushing, where someone reached out to me once, traced the trapped flute of my collarbone. I never saw that man's face, only the gold-rimmed glasses floating in the fog. And then the feeling, the velvet heat of it, everywhere inside me.

Is that what art is? To be touched thinking what we feel is ours when, in the end, it was someone else, in longing, who finds us?

When Houdini failed to free himself from his handcuffs at the London Hippodrome, his wife, Bess, gave him a long, deep kiss. In doing so, she passed him the key that would save him.

If there's a heaven I think it looks like this.

For no reason, I Googled Trevor's name the other day. The White Pages say he's still alive, that he's thirty years old and lives only 3.6 miles from me.

The truth is memory has not forgotten us.

A page, turning, is a wing lifted with no twin, and therefore no flight. And yet we are moved.

While cleaning my closet one afternoon I found a Jolly Rancher in the pocket of an old Carhartt jacket. It was from Trevor's truck. He always kept them in his cup holder. I unwrapped it, held it between my fingers. The memory of our voices is inside it. "Tell me what you know," I whispered. It caught the light from the window like an ancient jewel. I went inside the closet, closed the door, sat down in the tight dark, and placed the candy, smooth and cool, in my mouth. Green Apple.

I'm not with you because I'm at war with everything but you.

A person beside a person inside a life. That's called parataxis. That's called the future.

We're almost there.

I'm not telling you a story so much as a shipwreck—the pieces floating, finally legible.

Head around the bend, past the second stop sign with "H8" spray-painted in white on the bottom. Walk toward the white house, the one with its left side charcoal-grey with exhaust blown from the scrapyard across the highway.

There's the upstairs window where, one night when I was little, I woke to a blizzard outside. I was five or six and didn't know things ended. I thought the snow would continue to the sky's brim—then beyond, touching god's fingertips as he dozed in his reading chair, the equations scattered across the floor of his study. That by morning we would all be sealed inside a blue-white stillness and no one would have to leave. Ever.

After a while, Lan found me, or rather her voice appeared beside my ear. "Little Dog," she said as I watched the snow, "you want to hear a story? I tell you a story." I nodded. "Okay," she went on, "long ago. One woman hold her daughter, like this," she squeezed my shoulders, "on a dirt road. This girl, name Rose, yes, like flower. Yes, this girl, her name Rose, that's my baby. . . . Okay, I hold her, my daughter. Little Dog," she shakes me, "you know her name? It's Rose, like flower. Yes, this little girl I hold in dirt road. Nice girl, my baby, red hair. Her name is. . . ." And we went on like that, till the street below glowed white, erasing everything that had a name.

What were we before we were we? We must've been standing by the shoulder of a dirt road while the city burned. We must've been disappearing, like we are now.

Maybe in the next life we'll meet each other for the first time—believing in everything but the harm we're capable of. Maybe we'll be the opposite of buffaloes. We'll grow wings and spill over the cliff as a generation of monarchs, heading home. Green Apple.

Like snow covering the particulars of the city, they will say we never happened, that our survival was a myth. But they're wrong. You and I, we were real. We laughed knowing joy would tear the stitches from our lips.

Remember: The rules, like streets, can only take you to *known* places. Underneath the grid is a field—it was always there—where to be lost is never to be wrong, but simply more.

As a rule, be more.

As a rule, I miss you.

As a rule, "little" is always smaller than "small." Don't ask me why.

I'm sorry I don't call enough.

Green Apple.

I'm sorry I keep saying *How are you?* when I really mean *Are you happy?*

If you find yourself trapped inside a dimming world, remember it was always this dark inside the body. Where the heart, like any law, stops only for the living.

If you find yourself, then congratulations, your hands are yours to keep.

Take a right on Risley. If you forget me, then you've gone too far. Turn back.

Good luck.

Good night.

Good lord, Green Apple.

The room is silent as a photograph. Lan is stretched out on the floor on a mattress. Her daughters—you and Mai—and I are by her side. Wrapped around her head and neck is a sweat soaked towel, making a hood that frames her skeletal face. Her skin had stopped trying, the eyes fallen into her skull, as if peering from inside the brain itself. She resembles a wood carving, shriveled and striated with deep lines. The only indication that she's alive is her favorite yellow blanket, now grey, rising and falling on her chest.

You say her name for the fourth time and her eyes open, searching each of our faces. On the nearby table, a pot of tea we forget to drink. And it was that floral, sweet jasmine scent that makes me aware, by contrast, of the caustic, acrid odor undercutting the air.

Lan has been lying in the same spot for two weeks. With the slightest movement shooting pain through her thin frame, she developed bedsores under her thighs and back that got infected. She has lost control over her bowels and the bedpan beneath her is perpetually half-full, her insides literally letting go of themselves. My stomach grabs as I sit, fanning her, her remaining strands of hair fluttering at her temples. She peers at each of us, again and again, as if waiting for us to change.

"I'm burning," she says, when she finally speaks. "I'm burning like a hut inside." Your voice, in reply, is the softest I've ever heard it. "We'll put water on it, Ma, okay? We're gonna put out the fire."

The day Lan was diagnosed, I stood in the doctor's nothing-white office as he spoke, his voice sounding underwater, pointing to various sections of my grandmother, her skeleton pinned against the backlit screen.

But what I saw was emptiness.

On the X-ray, I stared at the space between her leg and hip where the cancer had eaten a third of her upper femur and part of the socket, the ball completely gone, the right hip porous and mottled. It reminded me of a sheet of metal, rusted and corroded thin in a junkyard. There was no evidence as to where that part of her disappeared to. I looked closer. Where was the translucent cartilage, the marrow, the minerals, the salt and sinew, the calcium that once formed her bones?

I felt then, as the nurses droned on around me, a new and singular anger. My jaw and fists tensed. I wanted to know who did this. I needed this act to have an author, a consciousness held in a defined and culpable space. For once, I wanted, *needed,* an enemy.

Stage four bone cancer was the official diagnosis. While you waited in the hall with Lan in the wheelchair, the doctor handed me the manila envelope with the X-rays inside, and simply said, avoiding my gaze, to take your grandma home and give her whatever she wanted to eat. She had two weeks, maybe three.

We brought her home, laid her back on a mat on the tile floor where it was cool, placed pillows along her length to keep her legs in place. What made it worse, you remember, was that Lan had never once believed, even to the end, that she had a terminal illness. We explained her diagnosis to her, about the tumors, the cells, metastasis, nouns so abstract that we might as well have been describing witchcraft.

We told her that she was dying, that it would be two weeks, then one week, any day now. "Be ready. Be ready. What do you want? What do you need? What would you like to say?" we urged. But she wouldn't have it. She said we were just children, that we didn't know everything yet, and that when we grow up, we'd know how the world really works. And because denial, fabrication— storytelling—was her way of staying one step ahead of her life, how could any of us tell her she was wrong?

Pain, however, is no story in itself. And these last few days, while you were out making funeral arrangements, picking out the coffin, Lan would howl and cry out in long, piercing bursts. "What have I done?" she'd say, looking at the ceiling. "God, what have I done to have you step on me like this?" We would give her the synthetic Vicodin and OxyContin prescribed by the doctor, then the morphine, then more morphine.

I fanned her with a paper plate as she drifted in and out of consciousness. Mai, who had driven all night from Florida, shuffled through the rooms, cooking food and making tea in a zombie-like daze. Because Lan was too weak to chew, Mai would spoon oatmeal into her barely opened mouth. I kept fanning as Mai fed her, the two women, mother's and daughter's black hair fluttering in unison, their foreheads almost touching. A few hours later, you and Mai rolled Lan on her side and, with a rubber-gloved hand, removed the feces from your mother's body—too wasted to expel its own waste. I kept fanning her face, jeweled with sweat, her eyes shut as you worked. When it was over, she just lay there blinking.

I asked her what she was thinking. As if waking from a sleepless dream, she answered in a gutted monotone. "I used to be a girl, Little Dog. You know?"

"Okay, Grandma, I know—" But she wasn't listening.

"I used to put a flower in my hair and walk in the sun. After big rain, I walk in the sun. The flower I put on my ear. So wet, so cool." Her eyes drifted from me. "It's a stupid thing." She shook her head. "Stupid thing. To be a girl." After a while, she turned back to me as if remembering I was there. "You eat yet?"

We try to preserve life—even when we know it has no chance of enduring its body. We feed it, keep it comfortable, bathe it, medicate it, caress it, even sing to it. We tend to these basic functions not because we are brave or selfless but because, like breath, it is the most fundamental act of our species: to sustain the body until time leaves it behind.

I'm thinking now of Duchamp, his infamous *"sculpture."* How by turning a urinal, an object of stable and permanent utility, upside down, he radicalized its reception. By further naming it *Fountain,* he divested the object of its intended identity, rendering it with an unrecognizable new form.

I hate him for this.

I hate how he proved that the entire existence of a thing could be changed simply by flipping it over, revealing a new angle to its name, an act completed by nothing else but gravity, the very force that traps us on this earth.

Mostly, I hate him because he was right.

Because that's what was happening to Lan. The cancer had refigured not only her features, but the trajectory of her being. Lan, turned over, would be dust the way even the word *dying* is nothing like the word *dead*. Before Lan's illness, I found this act of malleability to be beautiful, that an object or person, once upturned, becomes more than its once-singular self. This agency for evolution, which once made me proud to be the queer yellow faggot that I was and am, now betrays me.

Sitting with Lan, my mind slides, unexpectedly, to Trevor. Trevor who by then had been dead just seven months. I think of the first time we had sex, not with his cock in my palm like we usually did, but for real. It was the September after my second season on the farm.

The crop was all hung, packed from beam to beam to the rafters, their leaves already wrinkled, the green, once deep and lush in the fields, now dulled to the shade of old uniforms. It was time to fire the coals and speed the curing process. This required that someone stay all night in the barn, burning briquettes piled in tin pie plates set eight or ten feet apart across the dirt floor. Trevor had asked me to come hang out for the night while he stoked the coals. All around us the heaps burned, glowing red and flickering each time a draft made its pass through the slats. The sweet scent swelled as the heat warped its way toward the roof.

It was past midnight by the time we found ourselves on the barn's floor, the oil lamp's gold halo holding off the dark around us. Trevor leaned in. I parted my lips in anticipation but he left them untouched, going lower this time, until his teeth grazed the skin below my neck. This was before I knew how far into the year those incisors would sink, before I knew the heat in that boy's marrow, his knuckled American rage, his father's inclination for weeping on the front porch after three Coronas while the Patriots crackled on the radio and a hardback of Dean Koontz's *Fear Nothing* sat by his side, before the old man found Trevor passed out in the Chevy's truck bed in a thunderstorm, the water lapping at his boy's ears as he dragged him through the mud, the ambulance, the hospital room, the heroin hot in Trevor's veins. Before he would come out of the hospital, clean for a whole three months before hitting it again.

The air, close and thick from the summer's last heat, whistled low through the barn. I pressed myself into his sunbaked skin, still warm from the day in the field. His teeth, ivory and unrotted, nibbled my chest, nipples, stomach. And I let him. Because nothing could be taken from me, I thought, if I had already given it away. Our clothes fell off us like bandages.

"Let's just do it." On top of me, his voice strained as he struggled to kick off his boxers.

I nodded.

"I'll be slow, okay?" His mouth a gash of youth. "I'll be easy."

I turned—tentative, thrilled—toward the dirt floor, planted my forehead on my arm, and waited.

My shorts at my ankles, Trevor postured up behind me, his pubes brushing against me. He spat several times into his hand, rubbed the spit between my legs until everything was thick and slick and undeniable.

I put my head back down. The scent of dirt from the barn floor, notes of spilled beer and iron-rich soil as I listened to the wet clicks of his cock as he stroked his spit along its length.

When he pushed I felt myself scream—but didn't. Instead, my mouth was full of salted skin, then the bone underneath as I bit down on my arm. Trevor stopped, not yet all the way in, sat up, and asked if I was okay.

"I dunno," I said into the floor, panting.

"Don't cry on me again. Don't you cry on me now." He spat another wad, let it fall on his length. "Let's try again. If it's bad we'll stop for good."

"Okay."

He pushed, deeper this time, pushed his weight down hard—and slid inside me. The pain sparked white in the back of my head. I bit down, my wrist bone touched the contours of my teeth.

"I'm in. I'm in, little man." His voice cracked into the whisper-shout terror of a boy who got exactly what he wanted. "I'm in," he said, astonished. "I can feel it. Fuck. Oh fuck."

I told him to hold still as I braced against the dirt floor and gathered myself. The pain shot out from between my legs.

"Let's keep going," he said. "I gotta keep going. I don't wanna stop."

Before I could respond he was pumping again, his arms planted on each side of my head, the heat pulsing from them as he worked. He was wearing his gold cross, the one he never takes off, and it kept poking at my cheek. So I took it in my mouth to keep it steady. It tasted like rust, salt, and Trevor. The sparks in my head bloomed with each thrust. After a while, the pain melted into a strange ache, a weightless numbness that swept through me like a new, even warmer season. The feeling brought on, not by tenderness, as from caress, but by the body having no choice but to accommodate pain by dulling it into an impossible, radiating pleasure. Getting fucked in the ass felt good, I learned, when you outlast your own hurt.

What Simone Weil said: *Perfect joy excludes even the very feeling of joy, for in the soul filled by the object, no corner is left for saying "I."*

As he heaved above me I unconsciously reached back to touch myself, to make sure I was still there, still me, but my hand found Trevor instead—as if by being inside me, he was this new extension of myself. The Greeks thought sex was the attempt of two bodies, separated long ago, to return to one life. I don't know if I believe this but that's what it felt like: as if we were two people mining one body, and in doing so, merged, until no corner was left saying *I*.

Then, about ten minutes in, as Trevor went faster, our skin sucking with humid sweat, something happened. A scent rose up to my head, strong and deep, like soil, but sharp with flaw. I knew right away what it was, and panicked. In the heat of it, I didn't think, didn't yet know how to prepare myself. The porn clips I had seen never showed what it took to arrive where we were. They just did it—quick, immediate, sure, and spotless. No one had shown us how this was to be done. No one had taught us how to be this deep—and deeply broken.

Ashamed, I pressed my forehead to my wrist and let it throb there. Trevor slowed, then paused.

All quiet.

Above us the moths flitted between the tobacco. They had come to feed on the plants, but the pesticides left over from the fields killed them soon as they placed their mouths on the leaves. They fell all around us, their wings, in the midst of death throes, buzzed across the barn floor.

"Fuck." Trevor stood up, his face disbelieving.

I turned away. "Sorry," I said instinctually.

His cock, touched at the tip with the dark inside me, pulsed under the lamplight as it softened. I was, in that moment, more naked than I was with my clothes off—I was inside out. We had become what we feared most.

He breathed hard above me. Trevor being who he was, raised in the fabric and muscle of American masculinity, I feared for what would come. It was my fault. I had tainted him with my faggotry, the filthiness of our act exposed by my body's failure to contain itself.

He stepped toward me. I rose to my knees, half covered my face, bracing.

"Lick it up."

I flinched.

Sweat shone on his forehead.

A moth, suffocating, thrashed against my right knee. Its huge and final death merely a quiver on my skin. A breeze shifted the dark outside. A car hummed down the road across the fields.

He gripped my shoulder. How did I already know he would re-act like this?

I twisted my face to meet him.

"I said get up."

"What?" I searched his eyes.

I had misheard.

"C'mon," he said again. "Get the hell up."

Trevor pulled me by the arm to my feet. We stepped out of the oil lamp's gold circle, leaving it empty and perfect again. He led me, along the barn, his grip tight. The moths dipped in and out between us. When one hit my forehead and I stopped, he yanked and I stumbled behind him. We reached the other side, then through the door, into the night. The air was cool and starless. In the sudden dark, I made out only his pale back, grey-blue in the un-light. After a few yards, I heard the water. The river's current, although gentle, frothed white around his thighs. The crickets grew louder, lush. The trees rustled unseen in the massed shadows across the river. Then Trevor let go, dipped under, before quickly surfacing. Droplets ran down his jaw, tinkled around him.

"Clean yourself," he said, his tone oddly tender, almost frail. I pinched my nose and dunked under, gasping from the cold. In an hour, I'll be standing in our dim kitchen, the river still damp in my hair, and Lan will shuffle into the glow of the night-light above the stove. *I won't tell anyone you been at sea, Little Dog.* She will put her finger over her lips and nod. *This way, the pirate spirits won't follow you.* She will take a dishrag and dry my hair, my neck, pausing over the hickey that, by then, will be the shade of dried blood under my jaw. *You been far away. Now you home. Now you dry,* she will say as the floorboards creak under our shifting weight.

The river up to my chest now, I waved my arms to keep steady. Trevor put his hand on my neck and we stood, quiet for a moment, our heads bent over the river's black mirror.

He said, "Don't worry about that. You heard?"

The water moved around me, through my legs.

"Hey." He did that thing where he made a fist under my chin and tilted my head up to meet his gaze, a gesture that would usually get me to smile. "You heard me?"

I just nodded, then turned to shore. I was only a few steps ahead of him before I felt his palm push hard between my shoulders, leaning me forward, my hands instinctually braced on my knees. Before I could turn around, I felt his stubble, first between my thighs, then higher. He had knelt in the shallows, knees sunk in river mud. I shook—his tongue so impossibly warm compared to the cold water, the sudden, wordless act, willed as a balm to my failure in the barn. It felt like an appalling second chance, to be wanted again, in this way.

Far across the fields, just beyond a line of sycamores, a single lit window in the upstairs room of an old farmhouse flickered in the dark. Above it, a handful of straggling stars were biting through the sky's milky haze. He gripped my thighs with both hands, pressed me into him, to further prove the point. I stared at the water's convulsed shapes as I caught my breath. I looked between my legs and saw his chin moving to work the act into what it was, what it always has been: a kind of mercy. To be clean again. To be good again. What have we *become* to each other if not what we've *done* to each other? Although this was not the first time he did this, it was the only time the act gained new, concussive power. I was devoured, it seemed, not by a person, a Trevor, so much as by desire itself. To be reclaimed by that want, to be baptized by its pure need. That's what I was.

When he was finished, he wiped his mouth with the back of his arm, then mussed my hair before wading to shore. "Good as always," he said over his shoulder.

"Always," I repeated, as if answering a question, then headed for the barn, where, under the oil lamp's waning glow, the moths kept dying.

After breakfast, around ten, while I sit on the front porch reading, Mai grabs my arm. "It's time," she says. I blink. "She's going." We rush into the living room where you're already kneeling at Lan's side. She's awake and mumbling, her eyes roving under their half-shut lids. You run to grab bottles of aspirin and Advil from the cupboards. As if ibuprofen would do us any good now. But to you, it is *all* medicine—remedies that had worked before; why shouldn't they work now?

You sit beside your mother, your hands, finally empty, lie in your lap. Mai points to Lan's toes. "They're turning purple," she says with eerie calm. "The feet, they go first—and they're purple. Only a half hour now, at most." I watch Lan's life begin to recede from itself. *Purple,* Mai had said, but Lan's feet don't look purple to me. They're black, burnished brown at the tips of the toes, stone-dark everywhere else, save for the toenails, which had an opaque yellowish tint—like bone itself. But it's the word *purple,* and with it that lush deep hue, that floods me. That's what I see as I watch the blood pull out of Lan's black feet, the green surrounded by clusters of violet in my mind, and realize the word is dragging me into a memory. Years ago, when I was six or seven, while walking with Lan along a dirt path that hugged the highway off Church St., she abruptly stopped and shouted. I couldn't hear her over the traffic. She pointed out the chain-link fence that divided the interstate from the sidewalk, eyes pupil-wide. "Look, Little Dog!" I stooped down, examined the fence.

"I don't get it, Grandma. What's wrong?"

"No," she said, annoyed, "get up. Look past the fence—there—those purple flowers."

Just beyond the fence, on the highway side, lay a spill of violet wildflowers, each blossom no larger than a thumbnail with a tiny yellow-white center. Lan crouched, held my shoulders, leveling her eyes with mine, serious. "Will you climb it, Little Dog?" Her gaze narrowed in mock skepticism, waiting. Of course, I nodded eagerly. And she knew that I would.

"I'll boost you up and you just grab them quick, alright?" I latched on to the fence as she lifted my hips. After wavering a bit,

I made it to the top, straddled it. I looked down and immediately felt sick, the flowers somehow tiny, faint brushstrokes on a whir of green. The wind from the cars blasted my hair. "I don't know if I can!" I shouted, near tears. Lan grabbed my calf. "I'm right here. I won't let anything happen to you," she said over the traffic. "If you fall, I cut open the fence with my teeth and save you."

I believed her and jumped, landed in a roll, got up, and brushed myself off. "Get them by the roots with both hands." She grimaced as she clung to the fence. "You have to be quick or we'll get in trouble." I pulled one bush up after the other, the roots bursting from the dirt in ashy clouds. I tossed them over the fence, each passing car made a gust so strong I almost fell over. I pulled and pulled and Lan stuffed them all in a plastic 7-Eleven bag.

"Okay. Okay! That's good enough." She waved me back over. I leapt up the fence. Lan reached up and pulled me down into her arms, clutching me. She began to shudder, and not until she put me down did I realize she was giggling. "You did it, Little Dog! You're my flower hunter. The best flower hunter in USA!" She held up one of the bushes in the chalky ochre light. "These will be perfect on our windowsill."

It was beauty, I learned, that we risked ourselves for. That night, when you came home, you pointed at our harvest foaming across the brown, dirt-polluted windowsill, their tendrils lacing along the dining table, and asked, impressed, how we got them. Lan gave a dismissive wave, saying we had found them, thrown out on the curbside by a flower shop. I peered from my toy soldiers at Lan, who placed a finger over her lips and winked as you took off your coat, your back to us. Her eyes smiled.

I would never know those flowers by name. Because Lan never had one for them. To this day, every time I see small, purple flowers, I swear they're the flowers I had picked that day. But without a name, things get lost. The image, however, is clear. Clear and purple, the color that climbs now to Lan's shins as we sit, waiting for it to run through her. You stay close to your mother and brush away the hair matted on her emaciated, skullish face.

"What do you want, Ma?" you ask, your mouth at her ear. "What do you need from us? You can have anything."

Outside the window, the sky is a mocking blue.

"Rice," I remember Lan saying, her voice somewhere deep inside her. "A spoonful of rice." She swallows, takes another breath. "From Go Cong."

We eye each other—the request impossible. Still, Mai gets up and disappears behind the beaded kitchen curtain.

Half an hour later she kneels beside her mother, a steaming bowl of rice in her hand. She holds the spoon to Lan's toothless mouth. "Here, Ma," she says, stoic, "it's Go Cong rice, just harvested last week."

Lan chews, swallows, and something like relief spreads across her lips. "So good," she says, after her one and only bite. "So sweet. That's our rice—so sweet." She motions at something far away with her chin and dozes off.

Two hours later, she stirs awake. We crowd around her, hear the single deep inhale pull down her lungs, as if she was about to dive underwater, and then, that's it—no exhale. She simply stills, like someone had pressed pause on a movie.

I sit there as you and Mai, without hesitation, move about,

your arms hovering over your mother's stiff frame. I do the only thing I know. My knees to my chest, I start to count her purple toes. 1 2 3 4 5 1 2 3 4 5 1 2 3 4 5. I rock to the numbers as your hands float over the body, methodic as nurses doing rounds. Despite my vocabulary, my books, knowledge, I find myself folded against the far wall, bereft. I watch two daughters care for their own with an inertia equal to gravity. I sit, with all my theories, metaphors, and equations, Shakespeare and Milton, Barthes, Du Fu, and Homer, masters of death who can't, at last, teach me how to touch my dead.

After Lan is cleaned and changed, after the sheets removed, the bodily fluids scrubbed from the floor and the corpse—because that's what language dictates now: corpse instead of her—we gather again around Lan. With all your fingers, you pry open her stuck jaw, while on the other side, Mai slips Lan's dentures inside. But because rigor mortis has already set in, the jaws clamp down before the set of incisors can be secured and the dentures pop out, fall onto the floor with a hard clack. You let out a scream, which you quickly silence with a hand over your mouth. "Fuck," you say in rare English, "fuck fuck fuck." With the second attempt, the teeth click into place, and you fall back against the wall beside your gone mother.

Outside, a dump truck clanks and beeps its way down the block. A few pigeons gargle among the scattered trees. At the bottom of it all, you sit, Mai's head rested on your shoulders, your mother's body cooling a few feet away. Then, your chin turning into a peach pit, you lower your face into your hands.

Lan has been dead five months now, and for five months has sat in an urn on your bedside table. But today we're in Vietnam. Tien Giang Province, home of Go Cong District. It is summer. The rice paddies sweep out around us, endless and green as the sea itself.

After the funeral, after the monks in saffron robes chant and sing around her polished granite gravestone, the neighbors from the village with trays of food lifted over their heads, the ones with white hair who recall Lan's life here nearly thirty years ago, offer their anecdotes and condolences. After the sun dips under the rice fields and all that's left is the grave site, its dirt still fresh and damp at its edges, strewn with white chrysanthemums, I call Paul in Virginia.

He makes a request I don't expect, and asks to see her. I take my laptop and carry it the few yards toward the graves, close enough to the house to obtain three bars of Wi-Fi.

I stand, the laptop held out in front of me, and point Paul's face to Lan's grave, which is embossed with a photo of her when she was twenty-eight, roughly the age when they first met. I wait from behind the screen as this American veteran Skypes with his estranged Vietnamese ex-wife, just buried. At one point, I think the signal had cut out, but then I hear Paul blowing his nose, his sentences amputated, struggling through his goodbyes. He's sorry, he says to the smiling face on the grave. Sorry that he went back to Virginia in '71 after he received notice that his mother was ill. How it was all a ploy to get him home, how his mother faked her tuberculosis until weeks turned to months, until the war began to close and Nixon stopped deploying troops and Americans started pulling out. How all the letters Lan sent were intercepted by Paul's brother. How it wasn't until one day, months before Saigon fell, a

soldier, just home, knocked on his door and handed him a note
from Lan. How Lan and their daughters had to leave the capital
after the fall. How they'll write again. He said sorry that it took
so long. That by the time the Salvation Army called him to let
him know there was a woman with a marriage certificate with
his name on it looking for him in a Philippine refugee camp, it was
already 1990. He had, by then, been married to another woman
for over eight years. He says all this in a flood of stuttered
Vietnamese—which he picked up during his tour and kept at
through their marriage—until his words are barely coherent under his heaving.

A few children from the village had gathered at the edge of the
graves, their curious and perplexed stares hover on the periphery.
I must look strange to them, holding the pixelated head of a white
man in front of a row of tombs.

As I look at Paul's face on the screen, this soft-spoken man, this
stranger turned grandfather turned family, I realize how little I
know of us, of my country, any country. Standing by the dirt road,
not unlike the road Lan had once stood on nearly forty years earlier, an M-16 pointed at her nose as she held you, I wait until my
grandpa's voice, this retired tutor, vegan, and marijuana grower,
this lover of maps and Camus, finishes his last words to his first
love, then close the laptop.

In the Hartford I grew up in and the one you grow old in, we greet
one another not with "Hello" or "How are you?" but by asking,
our chins jabbing the air, "What's good?" I've heard this said in

other parts of the country, but in Hartford, it was pervasive. Among those hollowed-out, boarded buildings, playgrounds with barbed-wire fences so rusted and twisted out of shape they were like something made out of nature, organic as vines, we made a lexicon for ourselves. A phrase used by the economic losers, it can also be heard in East Hartford and New Britain, where entire white families, the ones some call *trailer trash,* crammed themselves on half-broken porches in mobile parks and HUD housing, their faces OxyContin-gaunt under cigarette smoke, illuminated by flashlights hung by fishing lines in lieu of porch lights, howling, "What's good?" as you walked by.

In my Hartford, where fathers were phantoms, dipping in and out of their children's lives, like my own father. Where grandmothers, abuelas, abas, nanas, babas, and ba ngoais were kings, crowned with nothing but salvaged and improvised pride and the stubborn testament of their tongues as they waited on creaking knees and bloated feet outside Social Services for heat and oil assistance smelling of drugstore perfume and peppermint hard candies, their brown oversized Goodwill coats dusted with fresh snow as they huddled, steaming down the winter block—their sons and daughters at work or in jail or overdosed or just gone, hitching cross-country on Greyhounds with dreams of kicking the habit, starting anew, but then ghosting into family legends.

In my Hartford, where the insurance companies that made us the big city had all moved out once the Internet arrived, and our best minds were sucked up by New York or Boston. Where everybody's second cousin was in the Latin Kings. Where we still sell Whalers jerseys at the bus station twenty years after the Whalers ditched this place to become the Carolina Hurricanes. Hartford of Mark Twain, Wallace Stevens, and Harriet Beecher Stowe, writers whose vast imaginations failed to hold, in either flesh or ink, bodies like ours. Where the Bushnell theatre, the Wadsworth Atheneum (which held the first retrospective on Picasso in America), were visited mostly by outsiders from the suburbs, who park their cars valet and hurry into the warm auditorium halogens before driving home to sleepy towns flushed with Pier 1 Imports and Whole Foods. Hartford, where we stayed when other Vietnamese immigrants fled to California or Houston. Where we made a kind of life digging in and out of one brutal winter after another, where nor'easters swallowed our cars overnight. The two a.m. gunshots, the two p.m. gunshots, the wives and girlfriends at the C-Town checkout with black eyes and cut lips, who return your gaze with lifted chins, as if to say, *Mind your business.*

Because being knocked down was already understood, already a *given,* it was the skin you wore. To ask *What's good?* was to move, right away, to joy. It was pushing aside what was inevitable to reach the exceptional. Not great or well or wonderful, but simply *good.* Because good was more often enough, was a precious spark we sought and harvested of and for one another.

Here, good is finding a dollar caught in the sewer drain, is when your mom has enough money on your birthday to rent a movie, plus buy a five-dollar pizza from Easy Frank's and stick eight candles over the melted cheese and pepperoni. Good is knowing there was a shooting and your brother was the one that came home, or was already beside you, tucked into a bowl of mac and cheese.

That's what Trevor said to me that night as we climbed out of the river, the black droplets dripping from our hair and fingertips. His arm slung across my shivering shoulder, he put his mouth to my ear and said, "You good. You heard, Little Dog? You good, I swear. You good."

After we put Lan's urn in the ground, polished her grave one last time with cloth rags soaked in wax and castor oil, you and I return to our hotel in Saigon. Soon as we enter the dingy room with its choking air conditioner, you turn off all the lights. I stop midstride, not sure what to make of the sudden dark. It's early afternoon and the motorbikes can still be heard honking and puttering on the street below. The bed creaks, you had sat down.

"Where am I?" you say. "Where is this?"

Not knowing what else to say, I say your name.

"Rose," I say. The flower, the color, the shade. "Hong," I repeat. A flower is seen only toward the end of its life, just-bloomed and already on its way to being brown paper. And maybe all names are illusions. How often do we name something after its briefest form? Rose bush, rain, butterfly, snapping turtle, firing squad, childhood, death, mother tongue, me, you.

Only when I utter the word do I realize that rose is also the past tense of rise. That in calling your name I am also telling you to get up. I say it as if it is the only answer to your question—as if a name is also a sound we can be found in. Where am I? Where am I? You're Rose, Ma. You have risen.

I touch your shoulder with the gentleness Trevor showed me back in the river. Trevor who, wild as he was, wouldn't eat veal, wouldn't eat the children of cows. I think now about those children, taken from their mothers and placed in boxes the size of their lives, to be fed and fattened into soft meat. I am thinking of freedom again, how the calf is most free when the cage opens and it's led to the truck for slaughter. All freedom is relative—you know too well—and sometimes it's no freedom at all, but simply the cage widening far away from you, the bars abstracted with distance but still there, as when they "free" wild animals into nature preserves only to contain them yet again by larger borders. But I took it anyway, that widening. Because sometimes not seeing the bars is enough.

For a few delirious moments in the barn, as Trevor and I fucked, the cage around me became invisible, even if I knew it was never gone. How my elation became a trap when I lost control of my inner self. How waste, shit, excess, is what binds the living, yet is always present and perennial in death. When the calves are finally butchered, surrendering their insides is often their final act, their bowels shocked from the sudden velocity of endings.

I squeeze your wrist and say your name.

I look at you and see, through the pitch dark, Trevor's eyes—Trevor whose face has, by now, already begun to blur in my mind—how they burned under the barn lamp as we dressed, shuddering quietly from the water. I see Lan's eyes in her last hours, like needful drops of water, how they were all she could move. Like the calf's wide pupils as the latch is opened, and it charges from its prison toward the man with a harness ready to loop around its neck.

"Where am I, Little Dog?" You're Rose. You're Lan. You're Trevor. As if a name can be more than one thing, deep and wide as a night with a truck idling at its edge, and you can step right out of your cage, where I wait for you. Where, under the stars, we see at last what we've made of each other in the light of long-dead things—and call it good.

I remember the table. I remember the table made of words given to me from your mouth. I remember the room burning. The room was burning because Lan spoke of fire. I remember the fire as it was told to me in the apartment in Hartford, all of us asleep on the hardwood floor, swaddled in blankets from the Salvation Army. I remember the man from the Salvation Army handing my father a stack of coupons for Kentucky Fried Chicken, which we called Old-Man Chicken (Colonel Sanders's face was plastered on every red bucket). I remember tearing into the crispy meat and oil like it was a gift from saints. I remember learning that saints were only people whose pain was notable, noted. I remember thinking you and Lan should be saints.

"Remember," you said each morning before we stepped out in cold Connecticut air, "don't draw attention to yourself. You're already Vietnamese."

It's the first day of August and the sky's clear over central Virginia, now thick with summer's growth. We're visiting Grandpa Paul to celebrate my graduating college the spring before. We're in the garden. The first colors of evening fall upon the wooden fence and everything ambers, as if we're in a snowglobe filled with tea. You're in front of me, walking away, toward the far fence, your pink shirt shifting in and out of the shade. It catches, then loses the shadows under the oaks.

I remember my father, which is to say I am putting him back together. I am putting him together in a room because there must have been a room. There must have been a square in which a life would occur, briefly, with or without joy. I remember joy. It was the sound of coins in a brown paper bag: his wages after a day scaling fish at the Chinese market on Cortland. I remember the coins spilling onto the floor, how we ran our fingers through the cold pieces, inhaling their copper promise. How we thought we were rich. How the thought of being rich was a kind of happiness.

I remember the table. How it must have been made of wood.

The garden is so lush it seems to pulse in the weak light. Vegetation fills every inch of it, tomato vines robust enough to hide the chicken wire they lean on, wheatgrass and kale crowded in galvanized tubs the size of canoes. The flowers I know now by name: magnolias, asters, poppies, marigolds, baby's breath—all of it, every shade equalized by dusk.

What are we if not what the light says we are?

Your pink shirt glows ahead of me. Crouched, your back poised as you study something on the ground between your feet. You brush your hair behind your ears, pause, study it closer. Only the seconds move between us.

A swarm of gnats, a veil suspended over no one's face. Everything here seems to have just finished overflowing, resting, at last, spent and spilled from the summer's frothing. I walk toward you.

I remember walking with you to the grocery store, my father's wages in your hands. How, by then, he had beaten you only twice—which meant there was still hope it would be the last. I remember armfuls of Wonder Bread and jars of mayo, how you thought mayo was butter, how in Saigon, butter and white bread were only eaten inside mansions guarded by butlers and steel gates. I remember everyone smiling back at the apartment, mayonnaise sandwiches raised to cracked lips. I remember thinking we lived in a sort of mansion.

I remember thinking this was the American Dream as snow crackled against the window and night came, and we lay down to sleep, side by side, limbs tangled as the sirens wailed through the streets, our bellies full of bread and "butter."

Inside the house, Paul is in the kitchen bent over a bowl of pesto: thick shiny basil leaves, machete-crushed garlic cloves, pine nuts, onions roasted till their gold edges blacken, and the bright scent of lemon zest. His glasses fog as he leans in, struggling to steady his arthritic hand as he pours the steaming pasta over the mixture. A few gentle tosses with two wooden spoons and the bow ties are bathed in a moss-green sauce.

The windows in the kitchen sweat, replacing the view of the garden with an empty movie screen. It is time to call the boy and his mother in. But Paul lingers for a while, watches the blank canvas. A man with nothing, finally, in his hands, waiting for everything to start.

I remember the table, which is to say I am putting it together. Because someone opened their mouth and built a structure with words and now I am doing the same each time I see my hands and think *table,* think *beginnings.* I remember running my fingers along the edges, studying the bolts and washers I created in my mind. I remember crawling underneath, checking for chewed gum, the names of lovers, but finding only bits of dried blood, splinters. I remember this beast with four legs hammered out of a language not yet my own.

A butterfly, pinked by the hour, lands on a blade of sweetgrass, then flits off. The blade twitches once, then stills. The butterfly tumbles the length of the yard, its wings resembling that corner of Toni Morrison's *Sula* I dog-eared so many times the tiny ear broke off one morning in New York, fluttered down the liquid winter avenue. It was the part where Eva pours gasoline on her drug-doomed son and lights the match in an act of love and mercy I hope to both be capable of—and never know.

I squint. It's not a monarch—just a weak white blur ready to die in the first frost. But I know the monarchs are close by, their orange-and-black wings folded, dusted, and baked by heat, ready to flee south. Strand by strand twilight stitches our edges deep red.

One night back in Saigon, two days after we buried Lan, I heard the sound of tinny music and the pitched voice of children through the hotel balcony. It was nearly two in the morning. You were still asleep on the mattress beside me. I got up, slipped on my sandals, and walked out. The hotel was in an alley. My eyes adjusting to the fluorescent tube lights hung along the wall, I made my way toward the music.

The night blazed up before me. People were suddenly everywhere, a kaleidoscope of colors, garments, limbs, the glint of jewelry and sequins. Vendors were selling fresh coconuts, cut mangoes, rice cakes pressed into gooey masses wrapped in banana leaves and steamed in large metal vats, sugarcane juice sold in sandwich bags cut at the corners, one of them now held by a boy who sucked from the plastic, beaming. A man, his arms nearly black from sun, squatted in the street. He worked over a cutting board no larger than his palm, halved a roasted chicken with a single deft cleaver blow, then distributed the slippery pieces to a flock of waiting kids.

Between string lights hung low from balconies on each side of the street, I glimpsed a makeshift stage. On it, a group of elaborately dressed women gyrated, their arms colorful banners in the

breeze, singing karaoke. Their voices broke off and floated down
the street. Nearby, a small TV, propped on a plastic white dining
table, displayed the lyrics to a Vietnamese pop song from the
eighties.

You're already Vietnamese.

I hovered closer, still dazed from sleep. It seemed the city had
forgotten the time—or rather, forgotten time itself. From what
I knew there was no holiday, no occasion for jubilation. In fact,
just beyond the street, where the main road began, the roads
were empty, quiet as they should've been at that hour. All the
commotion was contained on a single block. Where people now
laughed and sang. Children, some young as five, ran through
swaying adults. Grandmothers in paisley and floral pajamas sat
on plastic footstools by doorways chewing on toothpicks, whose
heads stopped bobbing to the music only to shout at the kids
around them.

In the ground, Lan is *already Vietnamese.*

It was only when I came close enough to see their features, the
jutted and heavy jawlines, the low forward brows, did I realize the
singers were in drag. Their sequined outfits of varying cuts and
primary colors sparkled so intensely it seemed they were donning
the very reduction of stars.

I remember my father, which is to say I am cuffing him with
these little words. I am giving him to you with hands behind his
back, his head ducking into the patrol car because like the table,
this was how it was given to me: from mouths that never articu-
lated the sounds inside a book.

To the right of the stage were four people with their backs to everyone else. Heads bowed, they were the only ones not moving— as if enclosed in an invisible room. They stared at something on a long plastic table in front of them, their heads so low they looked decapitated. After a while, one of them, a woman with silver hair, rested her head on the shoulder of a young man to her right—and began to weep.

I remember getting a letter from my father while he was in prison, the envelope wrinkled, torn at the edges. I remember holding up a piece of paper covered with lines and lines whited out where the prison guards censored his words. I remember scraping at the chalky film that lay between my father and me. Those words. Nuts and bolts to a table. A table in a room with no people.

I stepped closer, and that's when I saw on the table, impossibly still, the distinct form of a body covered in a white sheet. By now all four mourners were openly weeping while, on stage, the singer's falsetto cut through their racked sobs.

Nauseous, I searched the starless sky. A plane blinked red, then white, then blurred behind a band of clouds.

I remember studying my father's letter and seeing a scatter of tiny black dots: the periods left untouched. A vernacular of silence. I remember thinking everyone I ever loved was a single black dot on a bright page. I remember drawing a line from one dot to another with a name on each one until I ended with a family tree that looked more like a barbed-wire fence. I remember tearing it to shreds.

Later, I would learn that this was a common scene on a Saigon night. City coroners, underfunded, don't always work around the clock. When someone dies in the middle of the night, they get trapped in a municipal limbo where the corpse remains inside its death. As a response, a grassroots movement was formed as a communal salve. Neighbors, having learned of a sudden death, would, in under an hour, pool money and hire a troupe of drag performers for what was called "delaying sadness."

In Saigon, the sound of music and children playing this late in the night is a sign of death—or rather, a sign of a community attempting to heal.

It's through the drag performers' explosive outfits and gestures, their overdrawn faces and voices, their tabooed trespass of gender, that this relief, through extravagant spectacle, is manifest. As much as they are useful, paid, and empowered as a vital service in a society where to be queer is still a sin, the drag queens are, for as long as the dead lie in the open, an othered performance. Their presumed, reliable fraudulence is what makes their presence, to the mourners, necessary. Because grief, at its worst, is unreal. And it calls for a surreal response. The queens—in this way—are unicorns.

Unicorns stamping in a graveyard.

I remember the table. How flames started to lick at its edges.

I remember my first Thanksgiving. I was at Junior's house. Lan had made me a plate of fried eggrolls to bring over. I remember a house filled with over twenty people. People who slapped the table when they laughed. I remember food being piled on my plate: mashed potatoes, turkey, cornbread, chitlins, greens, sweet potato pie, and—eggrolls. Everyone praising Lan's eggrolls as they dipped them in gravy. How I, too, dipped them in gravy.

I remember Junior's mother putting a black plastic circle on a wooden machine. How the circle spun and spun until music happened. How music was the sound of a woman wailing. How everyone closed their eyes and tilted their heads as if listening to a secret message. I remember thinking I'd heard this before, from my mother and grandmother. Yes. I heard this even inside the womb. It was the Vietnamese lullaby. How every lullaby began with wailing, as if pain could not exit the body any other way. I remember swaying while listening to my grandmother's voice crooning through the machine. How Junior's father slapped me on the shoulder. "What you know about Etta James?" I remember happiness.

I remember my first year in an American school, the trip to the farm, how afterward, Mr. Zappadia gave each student a ditto of a black-and-white cow. "Color in what you saw today," he said. I remember seeing how sad the cows were at the farm, their large heads lulled behind electric fences. And because I was six, I remember believing color was a kind of happiness—so I took the brightest shades in the crayon box and filled my sad cow with purple, orange, red, auburn, magenta, pewter, fuchsia, glittered grey, lime green.

I remember Mr. Zappadia shouting, his beard trembling above me as a hairy hand grabbed my rainbow cow and crushed it in its fingers. "I said color in what you *saw*." I remember doing it over. I remember leaving my cow blank and staring out the window. How the sky was blue and merciless. How I sat there, among my peers— unreal.

In that street, beside the lifeless person who was somehow more animated in stillness than the living, the perpetual stench of sewage and runoff that lined the gutters, my vision blurred, the colors pooled under my lids. Passersby offered sympathetic nods, thinking I was part of the family. As I rubbed my face, a middle-aged man gripped my neck, the way Vietnamese fathers or uncles often do when trying to pour their strength into you. "You'll see her again. Hey, hey," his voice croaked and stung with alcohol, "you gonna see her." He slapped the back of my neck. "Don't cry. Don't cry."

·

This man. This white man. This Paul who swings open the wooden garden gate, the metal latch clanking behind him, is not my grandfather by blood—but by action.

Why did he volunteer in Vietnam when so many boys were heading to Canada to dodge the draft? I know he never told you— because he would have had to explain his abstract and implacable love of the trumpet in a language he would falter in. How he wanted, as he claimed, to be "a white Miles Davis" from the back-woods and cornfields of rural Virginia. How the trumpet's fat notes reverberated through the two-story farmhouse of his boy-hood. The one with its doors torn clean off by a father who raged through the rooms terrorizing his family. The father whose only connection to Paul was metal: the shell lodged in his old man's brain from the day he stormed Omaha beach; the brass Paul lifted to his mouth to make music.

I remember the table. How I tried to give it back to you. How you held me in your arms and brushed my hair, saying, "There, there. It's okay. It's okay." But this is a lie.

It went more like this: I gave you the table, Ma—which is to say I handed you my rainbow cow, pulled out of the wastebasket when Mr. Zappadia wasn't looking. How the colors moved and crinkled in your hands. How I tried to tell you but did not have the language you would understand. Do you understand? I was a gaping wound in the middle of America and you were inside me asking, *Where are we? Where are we, baby?*

I remember looking at you for a long time and, because I was six, I thought I could simply *transmit* my thoughts into your head if I stared hard enough. I remember crying in rage. How you had no idea. How you put your hand underneath my shirt and scratched my back anyways. I remember sleeping like that, calmed—my crushed cow expanding on the nightstand like a slow-motion color bomb.

Paul played music to get away—and when his old man tore up his application for music school, Paul got even further, all the way to the enlistment office, and found himself, at nineteen, in South East Asia.

They say everything happens for a reason—but I can't tell you why the dead always outnumber the living.

I can't tell you why some monarchs, on their way south, simply stop flying, their wings all of a sudden too heavy, not entirely their own—and fall away, deleting themselves from the story.

I can't tell you why, on that street in Saigon, as the corpse lay under the sheet, I kept hearing, not the song in the drag singer's throat, but the one inside my own. *"Many men, many, many, many, many men. Wish death 'pon me."* The street throbbed and spun its shredded colors around me.

In the commotion, I noticed the body had shifted. The head fell to one side, pulling the sheet with it and revealing the nape of a neck—already pale. And there, just under the ear, no larger than a fingernail, a jade earring dangled, then stopped. *"Lord I don't cry no more, don't look to the sky no more. Have mercy on me. Blood in my eye dawg and I can't see."*

I remember you grabbing my shoulders. How it was pouring rain or it was snowing or the streets were flooded or the sky was the color of bruises. And you were kneeling on the sidewalk tying my powder-blue shoes, saying, "Remember. Remember. You're already Vietnamese." You're already. You're all ready.

Already gone.

I remember the sidewalk, how we pushed the rusty cart to the church and soup kitchen on New Britain Ave. I remember the sidewalk. How it started to bleed: little drops of rouge appearing beneath the cart. How there was a trail of blood ahead of us. And behind us. Someone must have been shot or stabbed the night before. How we kept going. You said, "Don't look down, baby. Don't look down." The church so far away. The steeple a stitch in the sky. "Don't look down. Don't look down."

I remember Red. Red. Red. Red. Your hands wet over mine.

Red. Red. Red. Red. Your hand so hot. Your hand my own. I remember you saying, "Little Dog, look up. Look up. See? Do you see the birds in the trees?" I remember it was February. The trees were black and bare against an overcast sky. But you kept talking: "Look! The birds. So many colors. Blue birds. Red birds. Magenta birds. Glittered birds." Your finger pointed to the twisted branches. "Don't you see the nest of yellow chicks, the green mother feeding them worms?"

I remember how your eyes widened. I remember staring and staring at the end of your finger until, at last, an emerald blur ripened into realness. And I saw them. The birds. All of them. How they flourished like fruit as your mouth opened and closed and the words wouldn't stop coloring the trees. I remember forgetting the blood. I remember never looking down.

Yes, there was a war. Yes, we came from its epicenter. In that war, a woman gifted herself a new name—Lan—in that naming claimed herself beautiful, then made that beauty into something worth keeping. From that, a daughter was born, and from that daughter, a son.

All this time I told myself we were born from war—but I was wrong, Ma. We were born from beauty.

Let no one mistake us for the fruit of violence—but that violence, having passed through the fruit, failed to spoil it.

Paul is behind me by the gate, clipping a bushel of mint leaves to garnish the pesto. His scissors snap at the stems. A squirrel hurries down from a nearby sycamore, stops at the base, sniffs the air, then doubles back, vanishing up the branches. You're just ahead as I approach; my shadow touches your heels.

"Little Dog," you say, without turning, the sun long gone from the garden, "come here and look at this." You point to the ground at your feet, your voice a whisper-shout. "Isn't this crazy?"

I remember the room. How it burned because Lan sung of fire, surrounded by her daughters. Smoke rising and collecting in the corners. The table in the middle a bright blaze. The women with their eyes closed and the words relentless. The walls a moving screen of images flashing as each verse descended to the next: a sunlit intersection in a city no longer there. A city with no name. A white man standing beside a tank with his black-haired daughter in his arms. A family sleeping in a bomb crater. A family hiding underneath a table. Do you understand? All I was given was a table. A table in lieu of a house. A table in lieu of history.

"There was a house in Saigon," you told me. "One night, your father, drunk, came home and beat me for the first time at the kitchen table. You were not born yet."

But I remember the table anyway. It exists and does not exist. An inheritance assembled with bare mouths. And nouns. And ash. I remember the table as a shard embedded in the brain. How some will call it shrapnel. And some will call it art.

I am at your side now as you point at the ground where, just beyond your toes, a colony of ants pours across the dirt patch, a flood of black animation so thick it resembles the shadow of a person that won't materialize. I can't make out the individuals—their bodies linked to one another in an incessant surge of touch, each six-legged letter dark blue in the dusk—fractals of a timeworn alphabet. No, these are not monarchs. They are the ones who, come winter, will stay, will turn their flesh into seeds and burrow deeper—only to break through the warm spring loam, ravenous.

I remember the walls curling like a canvas as the fire blazed. The ceiling a rush of black smoke. I remember crawling to the table, how it was now a pile of soot, then dipping my fingers into it. My nails blackening with my country. My country dissolving on my tongue. I remember cupping the ash and writing the words *live live live* on the foreheads of the three women sitting in the room. How the ash eventually hardened into ink on a blank page. How there's ash on this very page. How there's enough for everyone.

You straighten up, dust off your pants. Night drains all colors from the garden. We walk, shadowless, toward the house. Inside, in the glow of shaded lamps, we roll up our sleeves, wash our hands. We speak, careful not to look too long at one another— then, with no words left between us, we set the table.

I hear it in my dream. Then, eyes open, I hear it again—the low wail swooping across the razed fields. An animal. Always it is an animal whose pain is this articulate, this clear. I'm lying on the barn's cool dirt floor. Above me, rows of tobacco hang, their limbs brushing against one another in a lone draft—which means it's the third week of August. Through the slats, a new day, already thick with summer's heat. The sound comes back and this time I sit up. It's not until I see him that I know I'm fifteen again. Trevor's asleep beside me. On his side, his arm a pillow, he looks more lost in thought than in sleep. His breath slow and eased, cut with hints of the Pabst we drank a few hours ago; the empties lined along on the bench above his head. A few feet away lies the metal army helmet, tipped back, the morning light, powder blue, collected in the bowl.

Still in my boxers, I walk out into the vast haze. The howl returns, the sound deep and vacuous, as if it had walls, something you could hide in. It must be wounded. Only something in pain could make a sound you could enter.

I search the flattened fields; mist wafts across the brown and tarnished soil. Nothing. It must be coming from the next farm. I walk, the humidity rises, my temples itch with new sweat.

In the next field, the last of the tobacco, fat and dark green, a week away from harvest, rises on all sides—somehow higher than usual, their tips just above my head. There's the oak where we'll total the Chevy in two weeks. The crickets have yet to unhinge their legs and now serrate the dense air as I go deeper, stopping each time the bellow shoots up, louder, closer.

Last night, under the rafters, our lips raw and spent from use, we lay, breathing. The dark quiet between us, I asked Trevor what Lan had asked me the week before.

"You ever think about those buffaloes on the Discovery Channel? I mean, how they keep running off those cliffs?"

He turned to me, his lip-fuzz brushed my arm. "The buffaloes?"

"Yeah, how come they keep running like that, even after the ones in front of them fall off? You'd think one of them would stop, would turn around."

His hand, tanned by work, was surprisingly dark on his stomach. "Yeah. I seen 'em on the nature shows. They just tumble off like a load of bricks. Right down." He clicked his tongue in disgust but his voiced dropped off. "Idiots."

We were still, letting the buffaloes go on falling, hundreds of them trotting silently down the cliffs in our heads. Somewhere in the next field, a pickup pulled into a driveway, gravel under the tires, a beam swung against the barn and lighted the dust above our noses, his shut eyes—eyes that I knew, by then, were no longer grey—but Trevor. The door slammed and someone came home and low voices could be heard, the single lilt of a question as it rose, "How was it?" or "Are you hungry?" Something plain and necessary, yet extra, with care, a voice like those tiny roofs over the phone booths along the train tracks, the ones made from the same shingles used for houses, except only four rows wide—just enough to keep the phone dry. And maybe that's all I wanted—to be asked a question and have it cover me, like a roof the width of myself.

"It's not up to them," Trevor said.

"What's not?"

"The damn buffaloes." He flicked the metal buckle on his belt. "It ain't up to them where they go. It's Mother Nature. She tells them to jump and they go on and do it. They don't got no choice about it. It's just the law of nature."

"The law," I repeated under my breath. "Like they're just following their loved ones, like their family's just going forward and they go with them?"

"Yeah, something like that," he said with sleepiness. "Like a family. A fucked family."

I felt this sudden surge of tenderness for him right then, a feeling so rare in me back then it felt like I was being displaced by it. Until Trevor pulled me back.

"Hey," he said, half-asleep, "what were you before you met me?"

"I think I was drowning."

A pause.

"And what are you now?" he whispered, sinking.

I thought for a second. "Water."

"Fuck off." He punched me on the arm. "And go to sleep, Little Dog." Then he grew quiet.

Then his eyelashes. You could hear them think.

I don't know what made me follow the hurt thing's voice, but I was pulled, as if promised an answer to a question I had not yet possessed. They say if you want something bad enough you'll end up making a god out of it. But what if all I ever wanted was my life, Ma?

I am thinking of beauty again, how some things are hunted because we have deemed them beautiful. If, relative to the history of our planet, an individual life is so short, a blink of an eye, as they say, then to be gorgeous, even from the day you're born to the day you die, is to be gorgeous only briefly. Like right now, how the sun is coming on, low behind the elms, and I can't tell the difference between a sunset and a sunrise. The world, reddening, appears the same to me—and I lose track of east and west. The colors this morning have the frayed tint of something already leaving. I think of the time Trev and I sat on the toolshed roof, watching the sun sink. I wasn't so much surprised by its effect—how, in a few crushed minutes, it changes the way things are seen, including ourselves—but that it was ever mine to see. Because the sunset, like survival, exists only on the verge of its own disappearing. To be gorgeous, you must first be seen, but to be seen allows you to be hunted.

I hear her call again, convinced now that it's a heifer. Ranchers often sell off the calves at night, ferrying them away on truck beds while the mothers slept in their stalls so they wouldn't wake up screaming for their babies. Some would wail so hard their throats would swell shut and a balloon had to be placed inside and inflated to expand the neck muscles.

I get closer. The tobacco stands high. When she wails again, the sound parts the stalks and the leaves shiver. I approach the small clearing where she is. The light froths blue over the plant tips. I hear her huge lungs working for air, soft but clear as wind. I part the thick-packed plants and step forward.

"Ma? Tell me the story again."

"I'm too tired, baby. Tomorrow. Back to sleep."

"I wasn't sleeping."

It's past ten and you're just back from the salon. You have a towel wrapped around your hair, your skin still warm from the shower.

"Come on, real quick. The one about the monkey."

You sigh, slipping under the blanket. "Alright. But get me a cigarette."

I take one from the carton on the nightstand, place it between your lips and light. You puff once, twice. I take it out, watch you.

"Okay, let's see. Once upon a time there was a Monkey King who—"

"No, Ma. The real one. Come on. Tell the real-life story."

I put the cigarette back in your mouth, let you puff.

"Okay." Your eyes search the room. "Once upon a time—scoot

closer, you wanna hear it or not? Once upon a time, in the old country, there were men who would eat the brains of monkeys."

"You were born in the Year of the Monkey. So you're a monkey."

"Yeah, I guess so," you whisper, staring far away. "I'm a monkey."

The cigarette smolders between my fingers.

Mist rises from the warm soil as I step through the crop. The sky widens, the tobacco drops off, revealing a circle no larger than god's thumbprint.

But nothing's here. No cow, no sound, only the last crickets, far off now, the tobacco still in the morning air. I stand, waiting for the sound to make me true.

Nothing.

The heifer, the farm, the boy, the wreck, the war—had I made it all up, in a dream, only to wake up with it fused to my skin?

Ma, I don't know if you've made it this far in this letter—or if you've made it here at all. You always tell me it's too late for you to read, with your poor liver, your exhausted bones, that after everything you've been through, you'd just like to rest now. That reading is a privilege you made possible for me with what you lost. I know you believe in reincarnation. I don't know if I do but I hope it's real. Because then maybe you'll come back here next time around. Maybe you'll be a girl and maybe your name will be Rose again, and you'll have a room full of books with parents who will read you bedtime stories in a country not touched by war. Maybe then, in that life and in this future, you'll find this book and you'll know what happened to us. And you'll remember me. Maybe.

For no reason, I start to run, past the clearing, back into the tobacco's stiff shade. My feet blurring into a small wind beneath me, I run. Even if no one I know is dead yet, not Trevor, not Lan, not my friends with the speed and heroin nowhere near their scarless veins. Even if the farm is not yet sold to make room for luxury condos, the barn not yet dismantled, its wood repurposed into craft furniture or to line the walls of trendy cafés in Brooklyn, I run.

I run thinking I will outpace it all, my will to change being stronger than my fear of living. My chest wet and leaf-raked, the day smoldering up at its edges, I push through so fast I feel like I've finally broken out of my body, left it behind. But when I turn around to see the panting boy, to forgive him, at last, for trying and failing to be good, there's no one there—only the full elms windless at the field's edge. Then, for no reason, I keep going. I think of the buffaloes somewhere, maybe in North Dakota or Montana, their shoulders rippling in slow motion as they race for the cliff, their brown bodies bottlenecked at the narrow precipice. Their eyes oil-black, the velvet bones of their horns covered with dust, they run, headfirst, together—until they become moose, huge and antlered, wet nostrils braying, then dogs, with paws clawing toward the edge, their tongues lapping in the light until, finally, they become macaques, a whole troop of them. The crowns of their heads cut open, their brains hollowed out, they float, the hair on their limbs fine and soft as feathers. And just as the first one steps off the cliff, onto air, the forever nothing below, they ignite into the ochre-red sparks of monarchs. Thousands of monarchs pour over the edge, fan into the white air, like a bloodjet hitting water. I race through the field as if my cliff was never written into this story, as if I was no heavier than the words in my name. And like a word, I hold no weight in this world yet still carry my own life. And I throw it ahead of me until what I left behind becomes exactly what I'm running toward—like I'm part of a family.

"Why didn't they get you then?" I place the Marlboro back in your mouth.

You hold my hand there for a while, breathe, then take it between your fingers. "Oh, Little Dog," you sigh. "Little Dog, Little Dog."

Monkeys, moose, cows, dogs, butterflies, buffaloes. What we would give to have the ruined lives of animals tell a human story—when our lives are in themselves the story of animals.

"Why didn't they get me? Well, 'cause I was *fast,* baby. Some monkeys are so fast, they're more like ghosts, you know? They just—*poof,*" you open your palm in a gesture of a small explosion, "disappear." Without moving your head, you look at me, the way a mother looks at anything—for too long.

Then, for no reason, you start to laugh.

The past tense of sing is not singed.

—Hoa Nguyen

Acknowledgments

On page 4, the line "Freedom . . . is nothing but the distance between the hunter and its prey" is from Bei Dao's poem "Accomplices" (*The August Sleepwalker*).

On page 33, the line "Two languages . . . beckoning a third" is paraphrased from *Roland Barthes* by Roland Barthes.

On page 187, the line "Too much joy, I swear, is lost in our desperation to keep it" is influenced by Zen Buddhist theory on joy and impermanence, as echoed by Max Ritvo in his 2016 interview with Divedapper.com.

I would like to thank a few people, in no particular order, who made me and my work possible in this world.

I'm indebted to the masterful journalism of Tom Callahan, whose in-depth reporting for *ESPN the Magazine* and *Golf Digest* broadened, enriched, and informed my understanding of Tiger Woods and his indelible legacy in golfing and American culture. Thanks to Elaine Scarry and her book, *On Beauty and Being Just*, for its intelligent, rigorous, and luminous complication of the subject.

To my teachers, for always seeing (and keeping) the road true: Roni Natov and Gerry DeLuca (Brooklyn College), Jen Bervin (Poets House), Sharon Olds (NYU), and my high school poetry teacher, Timothy Sanderson (Hartford County).

To Ben Lerner, without whom so much of my thinking and being as a writer would not be realized. Thank you for always reminding me that rules are merely tendencies, not truths, and genre borders only as real as our imaginations small. I am indebted to your big kindness, as well as the English Department at Brooklyn College, for granting me an emergency fund when I lost my housing the winter of 2009.

To Yusef Komunyakaa, thank you for showing me how to break the line and see the world more clearly at its brutal and inky joints. For tolerating my fanboying when, by luck, I sat down beside you one rainy night in a West Village theater, autumn 2008, and kept yapping about everything and nothing at all. I don't remember the movie but I'll never forget your laugh. Thank you for being my teacher.

A deep bow to the following artists and musicians whom I leaned on, repeatedly, while writing this book: James Baldwin, Roland Barthes, Charles Bradley, Thi Bui, Anne Carson, Theresa Hak Kyung Cha, Alexander Chee, Gus Dapperton, Miles Davis, Natalie Diaz, Joan Didion, Marguerite Duras, Perfume Genius, Thich Nhat Hanh, Whitney Houston, Kim Hyesoon, Etta James, Maxine Hong Kingston, King Krule, Lyoto Machida, MGMT, Qiu Miaojin, Mitski, Viet Thanh Nguyen, Frank Ocean, Jenny Offill, Frank O'Hara, Rex Orange County, Richard Siken, Nina Simone, Sufjan Stevens, and C. D. Wright.

To every Asian American artist who came before me, thank you.

For reading this book in manuscript form, for your gracious and lantern-like comments and insight, thanks to Peter Bienkowski, Laura Cresté, Ben Lerner (again), Sally Wen Mao, and Tanya Olson.

For your friendship, for sharing this art and air with me: Mahogany Browne, Sivan Butler-Rotholz, Eduardo C. Corral, Shira Erlichman, Peter Gizzi, Tiffanie Hoang, Mari L'Esperance, Loma (aka Christopher Soto), Lawrence Minh-Bùi Davis, Angel Nafis, Jihyun Yun.

To Doug Argue, your vibrant openness and courage helped me be braver with our truths and, in more ways than you know, made this book possible.

Thanks to my superb and fearless agent, Frances Coady (Captain Coady!), for your keen eyes, tireless faith, and patience, for respecting me as an artist first and foremost. For finding and believing in me before it all began.

Deep gratitude to my editor, Ann Godoff, for your pristine enthusiasm for this little book, for understanding it so thoroughly, so totally, and with bone-deep care. For standing behind its author's vision in every way. And to the superb team at Penguin Press: Matt Boyd, Casey Denis, Brian Etling, Juliana Kiyan, Shina Patel, and Sona Vogel.

I'm indebted to Dana Prescott and Diego Mencaroni of the Civitella Ranieri Foundation, where, during a power outage in an Umbrian thunderstorm, this book was started, by hand. And to Leslie Williamson and the Saltonstall Foundation for the Arts, where this book was finished. Generous support was also provided by the Lannan Foundation, the Whiting Foundation, and the University of Massachusetts–Amherst.

Thank you, Peter, always, for Peter.

Ma, cảm ơn.